Perimeter

John Reizer

ISBN 978-0-557-66775-8

Published by Lulu Press, Inc.

The characters and events in this book are fictitious. Any
similarity to real persons, living or dead, is coincidental and
not intended by the author.

Perimeter

John Reizer

John Reizer

Dedication

For Melissa and Kayla

John Reizer

About the Author

John Reizer lives in Spartanburg, South Carolina with his wife and daughter. He has been a practicing chiropractor for over 24 years.

John has published six bestselling books on the subject of chiropractic.

"Perimeter" is Dr. Reizer's third novel. Additional information is available at www.johnreizer.com.

Chapter One

Kyle Wilson was thoroughly exhausted. His career as a self-employed computer entrepreneur had turned out to be a lot more demanding than he, initially, thought. Although he enjoyed building intricate websites for his clients, the day-to-day pressures that went along with being a small business owner completely stressed him out.

Kyle had graduated from the University of South Carolina Upstate, two years earlier, where he earned a Bachelor's degree in computer sciences. His reputation, as a brilliant student, at the institution eventually opened an important door for him to land a good paying job in the school's information and technology department.

After working at the university for just over a year, Kyle learned that major budget cuts would prematurely end his employment at the state funded facility.

The deep economic recession, which began in 2008, had dragged on for over four years. It had adversely impacted many people's lives within the country and positions of employment, in general, were few and far between. Kyle decided that the solution to his problem lay in the creation of a home computer business.

Kyle quickly discovered that running a home-based business was a lot different than showing up to a 9 to 5 job, Monday thru Friday. Instead of having one boss, like he did at the university, he currently had dozens of clients constantly demanding a hundred percent of his time and attention, 24 hours a day.

Thank God it was finally Friday, he thought to himself. This day had started out, pretty much, as any other Friday. It was December 21, 2012, only four days remained until Christmas. Kyle's business had been on the upswing and he was really looking forward to a nice relaxing weekend. Maybe he'd catch a movie at the Regal 16 Theatre in nearby Spartanburg, or perhaps he'd just stay at home and catch up on some leisure reading. There was a very interesting article he'd begun to read and never quite had the chance to finish, for various reasons, in the December issue of *Time Magazine*. He'd definitely make it his top priority to finish reading that story over the weekend.

It was later that evening, however, when things started to happen that would separate this day from the likes of any other. It was about a quarter to 9 and Kyle had already cooked and finished eating his dinner. Like he did on most Friday evenings, the computer entrepreneur was propped up on his brown, Italian leather recliner. The new high definition flat screen TV he'd recently purchased from Sears had been playing the sci-fi movie, *Back to the Future,* in the far corner of the apartment. He'd purposely set the volume extremely low. Kyle had been focused on the laptop computer that was perched between his knees. He played the TV only to create some background noise, in the apartment, which seemed to comfort him during the evening hours.

On the other side of the living room was a small fiber optic Christmas tree. Although he hadn't placed any decorations on it, the holiday prop still managed to project a beautiful array of colors throughout the apartment. In some respects, the Christmas tree was very symbolic of Kyle's life. It looked good, offered some signs of hope, but was missing something important.

Kyle was 25 years old and still an eligible bachelor. It's not that he didn't like women. He just never seemed to have an opportunity to meet the right one. That was until two days earlier when he'd met the most beautiful young lady, he'd ever laid his eyes on, right inside his own apartment complex. Actually, he'd bumped into her by accident.

Kyle had needed to speak with the maintenance supervisor, Paul Callahan, about a leak in his bedroom closet. The supervisor usually camped out in a small utility shed that was located directly across from the rental office. Kyle figured that he'd kill two birds with one stone. He decided to pay next month's rent, after visiting the maintenance guy, so that he wouldn't have to make a second trip to the office, to write a check, the following week.

On the way out from paying the rent, Kyle collided with a young woman at the office front door. She had long, silky, black hair and olive colored skin. Her face was stunningly pretty.

It was a bit of an awkward scene. She'd been carrying some papers and a rather large hardcover book. Her belongings dropped onto the sidewalk during the collision. Kyle and the young woman quickly reached down, at the same time, and began picking up her things.

"I'm terribly sorry," he'd said. Kyle had noticed that the publication, resting on the ground, was a textbook titled, *The Fundamentals of Basic College English*. Nervously, he picked up the book and quickly handed it back to her. Then one of those uncomfortable moments occurred where he just stood there, staring at the angelic looking woman, without uttering a word. She was gorgeous and he definitely wanted to get to know her but he became completely tongue-tied. As usual, Kyle blew the chance encounter by leaving the scene without introducing himself. When he returned to his apartment, a short time later, he was very depressed that he hadn't been more aggressive with his opportunity.

Kyle had always been a bit of a loner and somewhat shy. Whenever he saw a young lady that he was attracted to, he seemed to always freeze up and lose his nerve. He just wouldn't allow himself the chance to strike up a conversation.

Kyle also hated going to the local night clubs, and wasn't much of a drinker. He preferred working out with weights, in his apartment, and avoiding the local fast food establishments. He knew that meeting a girl would be very challenging for him because he wasn't into the social scene.

Although he never thought so, Kyle was an exceptionally good looking young man. He possessed a finally chiseled face that favored the likes of a New York City model. He had long flowing blond hair along with beautiful golden eyelashes that further accentuated his good looks. And although he didn't realize it, many local women, he came into contact with, secretly admired his well defined and very athletic looking body.

On this particular evening, Kyle had been surfing the Internet for about forty minutes and was getting pretty tired when he'd suddenly, and without warning, heard a loud thunderous boom outside his single story apartment. It sounded, initially, like a beam, in the building's attic, had dislodged and fallen. The noise was followed by another; a screeching vibration that seemed to tear a massive hole in the Earth's atmosphere. It was an absolutely horrific sound. In fact, it reminded him of the sound a jet plane might make if it were hurtling towards the ground at breakneck speed.

Kyle immediately jumped off the recliner and tossed the laptop computer onto the chair. He quickly made his way to the apartment backdoor and looked up into the night sky. Outside, the entire area seemed to be bathed in an eerie shade of red. It was the most peculiar thing he'd ever witnessed. The strange color had completely engulfed the entire backyard area outside his apartment building. For as far and as long as Kyle could see, everything was bathed in a mysterious red hue.

And then it began! An event that would forever change his life and the lives of countless others was taking place outside his apartment. A magnificent flash of white light suddenly illuminated the sky. It was so brilliant that Kyle had to turn his head away from the window. He dove, headfirst, onto the apartment floor and immediately shut his eyes. The blinding light was accompanied by a tremendous amount of heat. Kyle desperately hugged the ground while keeping his eyes closed the entire time.

Chapter Two

October 31, 2000

The University of South Carolina – Spartanburg, SC

"Dr. Grossman! Dr. Paul Grossman, can I please speak with you for just a moment?" yelled the blond haired man as he sprinted across the faculty parking lot.

The 51 year old physics professor turned around, just in time, to see the approaching stranger dodge an oncoming car. He estimated the man to be in his early to mid 20's. He didn't recognize the individual's face, but assumed that he was enrolled in one of his general physics courses. "Do I know you?" the professor asked.

Slightly out of breath from running, the stranger placed both his hands on the top of his knees as he attempted to suck some air into his lungs. "I don't think that we've ever met before. My name is James Wilson."

"Well Mr. Wilson, what can I do for you today?" The professor stared at the young man curiously.

Paul Grossman wasn't a very distinguished looking fellow. He was dressed in a brown, slightly frayed, suit and was wearing a matching brown bowtie. Soaking wet, he weighed no more than 150 pounds. He had an oval shaped face, and a partially receding, gray hairline. He was clutching an older looking briefcase in his right hand.

"Professor, I flew into Greenville-Spartanburg this morning from Jacksonville, Florida. About two months ago, my parents, Kyle and Angel Wilson, were killed in an automobile accident just outside of Orlando."

The professor set down his briefcase onto the surface of the parking lot. He'd noticed that the blond haired young man was quite handsome. "I'm very sorry to hear that, James," he replied.

"Thanks. Look, the reason I'm here in Spartanburg, chasing after you in the parking lot, is because of an envelope that I found scattered among my parents' personal papers."

"An envelope?"

"Yes sir. And it was addressed to you." He handed the professor a very old and tattered piece of paper.

"When I originally found the document, it had another paper taped to it," James said. He was breathing easier now. "On it, my mother had written me specific instructions to hand deliver the parcel to you here at the university. She was especially clear about the fact that I was only supposed to deliver the envelope, to you, in the event that both my parents had passed away."

Paul felt his curiosity burn away all other consideration. He carefully opened the parcel and gently pulled out a white napkin and another smaller envelope that was still sealed. His eyes immediately moved to the second envelope which had the words; **TO BE OPENED—IN PRIVATE ONLY – BY DR. PAUL GROSSMAN**, printed on the front of it. Next, he glanced over at the napkin. On one side was a single sentence that was printed in blue, block letters. The sentence read:

KEEP SAFE AND DO NOT DESTROY!

Written on the napkin's flip side, also in blue ink, was a detailed schematic drawing of a circuit board. On the top of the napkin was a group of numbers and letters that read:

34.93 N 81.92 W: 122112: 20:45

The professor stared at the drawing and then at the long succession of numbers and letters. His eyes nearly jumped out of his head. He'd instantly observed that the content, on the paper napkin, had been written and drawn with his own hand.

Chapter Three

When he opened his eyes, Kyle didn't see a thing. It was completely dark in the apartment. He was seated in his recliner clutching the laptop. All the lights in the apartment were off. He wondered what had happened. A few seconds ago, he'd been on the apartment floor trying to hide from a brilliant flash of light. Now he found himself, back on the recliner, holding his computer.

Kyle gripped the laptop's frame and realized that it too had been turned off. He pushed the button to restart the machine, but nothing happened. Kyle pushed the recliner back to its normal position and picked himself off the chair. He carefully managed, in the absence of light, to make his way over to the nearest wall switch and flipped it on and off. Again, nothing happened. The power seemed to be out throughout the entire apartment.

Kyle cautiously moved over to the back door and peered outside again. It was pitch dark this time and there was no evidence, whatsoever, of the red glow, in the sky, which had been present just a few moments earlier. He wondered if he'd been dreaming. *That's what it must have been – a dream*, he thought to himself.

Kyle maneuvered his way over towards the kitchen where he kept a flashlight. He fumbled around in the darkness before he remembered it was positioned against the wall for emergencies such as this. Keeping his arms stretched out, Kyle finally made contact with the kitchen countertop and he was able to navigate his way towards the flashlight. He picked up the light and pushed in the switch. Nothing happened.

"God dammit," he said. "Nothing works when you need it to." He tossed the flashlight aside, hearing the sound of cracking plastic as it struck the kitchen floor.

Kyle reached for the telephone that was situated on the wall alongside of where the flashlight had been located. He wanted to place a call to Duke Energy to report the power outage. He lifted the receiver and placed it to his ear. No dial tone. "This is absolutely unbelievable!" He yelled the words out loud. Clearly frustrated with the night's turn of events, he slammed the phone back into its cradle.

A sudden knock on the apartment door startled him. "Just a moment," he called out as he began to feel his way towards the front door. Even though his eyes had begun to adjust to the darkened conditions, Kyle still found it a challenging proposition to find his way around the apartment. He immediately stubbed his left big toe on the corner of the refrigerator. "Ouch," he yelled and reached down to rub the affected area. Another knock on the door rattled through the small apartment. "I'm coming," he said raising his voice louder this time so that the person outside the apartment would definitely be able to hear him. Kyle cautiously made his way through the living room area and eventually located the front door.

Chapter Four

"What do you want?" Kyle yelled as he pressed his ear up against the door.

"My name is Angel McClure. I'm your new neighbor from across the hall."

When Kyle opened the door, he found himself standing face to face with the same beautiful, young brunette he'd bumped into at the rental office. She was holding a lighted candle in her hand. It fully illuminated the small area where the two of them were standing.

Kyle looked at her for a moment. Oddly enough, he didn't feel like he was at a sudden loss for words. "Hello, I'm Kyle Wilson." He stuck out his arm to shake her hand with a level of confidence that had previously escaped him. "I guess the entire building's out of power?"

Angel looked at Kyle. She'd recognized him right away. "You're the good looking guy that helped me pick up my papers the other day." She smiled as she reached out and shook his hand. "I just moved into F-12 yesterday afternoon." She brushed the hair away from her face. "Did you hear that loud bang before the lights went out?"

"Yeah," Kyle replied. "Did you happen to see the red sky?"

"Yes. Pretty creepy."

"I thought that maybe I'd been dreaming," Kyle explained, more confused now than he'd been a few minutes earlier.

"The lights and telephone aren't working at my place. I even tried three flashlights, and they didn't work either," Angel said. Her voice quivered a bit. "Nothing's working."

"Same thing here," Kyle explained. "Everything's dead!"

Angel, suddenly, looked back over her shoulder in the direction of the parking lot. She'd heard some voices and spotted a few dim lights that were moving about. "They seem to have lights that are working," she said.

Kyle stepped out of his apartment to get a better view of what Angel meant. The two of them decided to walk up to the parking area. As they got closer, Kyle and Angel were able to see that the people congregating in the parking lot were also using candles as a source for their lighting.

Kyle went up to one guy that had been clutching a small candle. "Hey," he yelled out to the man. "What's happening around here?"

The guy turned around and looked at Kyle. "Everything's fried is what's happening." He paused momentarily and looked up at the sky. "Anything that uses electric isn't working. We must've been hit with an EMP." The man, who seemed to be preoccupied with the strangeness of the current environment, walked away from Kyle and into the direction of some other people that were huddled together next to a garbage dumpster.

Kyle and Angel overheard two other men talking about a terrorist attack and some sort of invasion that, they believed, was taking place.

Angel tapped Kyle on the shoulder. "What's an EMP?"

"Electromagnetic pulse," he replied. "I think it's a type of military weapon that can be used to shoot a pulse of energy in different directions. It supposedly destroys the electronic components in most machines. I guess it makes everything that runs on electric, useless."

"Is that why the flashlights don't work?" Angel asked.

"Possibly," Kyle said. He looked up and down the parking area and out across the apartment complex. He could hear some people screaming and the sound of breaking glass in the distance. "I think we should get back inside our apartments where it's safe. We should wait for the lights to come back on before we go exploring any further."

Angel moved a bit closer to Kyle and said, "I'm really scared." She was sticking right by his side. "I know we just met, not even five minutes ago, but I really don't want to stay in my apartment, alone. Would you mind, terribly, if I camped out at your place until the morning?"

Again, in the distance, the unmistakable noise of breaking glass could be heard. It sounded as though a small riot was taking place on the other side of the apartment complex.

"No, I don't mind," Kyle said. "It's probably a good idea that we stick together until we figure out what's going on. Let's get back inside though. I don't like the sound of all the commotion out here."

Angel agreed. The two of them walked back down the sidewalk and made their way into Kyle's apartment. It was, apparently, going to be a very long evening.

Chapter Five

The darkness in Kyle's apartment was finally relieved by the presence of several large candles that he and Angel had strategically positioned in the kitchen and living room areas. Kyle had found the candles in the bedroom closet after remembering that he'd placed them there several weeks earlier. He'd purchased them at a Dollar General store awhile back because the power kept going off in his apartment. He didn't understand why, but Duke Energy had a difficult time keeping the apartment complex properly serviced without regular interruptions.

Several weeks earlier, he'd been knocked out of power, once again, due to an electrical storm. He'd used the candles then, and put them away in the closet after the power had been restored.

"That's a lot better," he said as he quickly surveyed the apartment. There was now an adequate level of lighting so that the two of them could manage to walk around without bumping into the furniture and other apartment fixtures.

Perimeter

Kyle glanced over at Angel from his position near the dining room table. She occupied the brown sofa alongside his leather recliner. He could tell that the young woman was tired and frightened. With better lighting in the room, he could also see that Angel was even prettier than he'd previously observed. She had a shapely figure and he guessed that she must have spent a lot of time in the gym. The flickering candlelight made the silhouette of her body seem to fade in and out of the darkness. Kyle knew that there was something extremely elegant about his new neighbor.

Although he tried his best to avoid constantly staring at her, he found Angel's beauty too difficult to ignore. Instead, he tried to observe her casually without drawing very much attention to the fact that he was actually checking her out. He didn't want to make her feel anymore uncomfortable than she already was from the situation that was taking place.

Angel smiled at Kyle. "I appreciate your letting me stay here tonight."

"I'm glad you're here," he replied.

"Kyle, what do you think is going on?"

Kyle walked over to the porch door and looked outside the window before he answered her. "I honestly don't know. But whatever's happening can't be too good."

Angel shifted her body into a more comfortable position on the sofa. "Do you have any family living here in the upstate?" she asked.

"No. My mom passed away several years ago from a heart attack. My dad left us when I was only two years old. I've never had the desire to try and find him. As far as I'm concerned, he's dead!" Kyle walked over and sat down on the recliner next to Angel.

"I'm really sorry to hear that," she said. There was a genuine sound of concern in her voice.

"It's okay," he assured her. "I've been a solo act for a long time. I'm used to this lifestyle."

"What about brothers or sisters?" Angel asked.

"No. I'm an only child."

"Do you have a girlfriend?"

"Not at the moment. I guess I'm a little too self-absorbed in my computer business. I don't really get a chance to socialize that much." Kyle paused for a moment and looked directly at her. "What about you? Are you married or do you have a significant other?"

Angel laughed softly. "No. I'm unattached as well. I've never known my biological parents. I was brought up in a few foster homes and, over the years, I've lost contact with those families."

"What do you do for a living, Angel?"

"I'm an assistant professor of English at the University of South Carolina, in Columbia. Actually, I'm on loan to the University of South Carolina Upstate for the next several semesters, so I'll be living here for about nine months."

"I'm hosting a professor. That's really impressive, Angel. You're a big shot!" Kyle had a wide grin stretched across his face.

"Assistant professor," she corrected him.

"It's still impressive," Kyle insisted.

"It helps me to pay the bills."

"Angel...," Kyle started to speak. He hesitated for a second as he stood up from the recliner. "...did you notice anything peculiar that might have happened right before the power went out?"

"What do you mean by peculiar?" she asked.

"Did you notice anything odd like maybe the sensation that there was a momentary lapse in time?"

Angel thought to herself for a second. "Now that you mention it, there was something weird that occurred." She placed her finger up against the side of her cheek. "When the bright light appeared, I was in the bedroom kneeling on my bed. I was looking out the window." She shifted her head slightly, her eyes looking up at the ceiling as she tried to recall the details as accurately as possible. "I don't remember walking from the bed to my desk. Yet, that's where I remember being after the power went off."

"Are you sure you don't remember walking over to the desk?" Kyle asked.

Angel was still attempting to piece together the unusual sequence of events. "No. I don't remember walking to the desk. I remember peeking out the bedroom window at the bright light. I was kneeling on the bed. I distinctly remember the lights going out and then I remember sitting at the desk. That's so damn strange."

"I'll say it's strange," Kyle said. "You know what else is strange?" He didn't give her a chance to answer the question. "The same thing, pretty much, happened to me. I was looking out the back window when the light occurred. I dove onto the floor and closed my eyes. I felt the heat, from the bright flash, hit the back of my body. When I opened my eyes, I was sitting on the recliner, holding the laptop." He was pointing to the chair.

Angel was still seated on the sofa, her legs folded beneath her. "There's got to be a logical explanation, Kyle."

"There's nothing logical about any of this," he replied. "Neither one of us can recall how we, suddenly, ended up at different locations within our apartments. The entire night is totally illogical!"

Angel's facial expression changed from looking puzzled to looking scared. "Kyle, do you think we've been nuked, or something catastrophic has happened?"

"I don't know, Angel. Hopefully, we'll find out some answers in the morning. Right now we should think about getting some rest. I'm going to let you sleep in my room and I'll stretch out here on the recliner."

Angel immediately protested. "Absolutely not! I want you to sleep in your room. I'll be fine right here, on the sofa. And, please, don't argue with me because I'm not going to change my mind."

Kyle grinned. "Suit yourself. If you get hungry or thirsty, there's bottled water, bananas, and some packages of dried fruit in the kitchen. Feel free to help yourself to anything in the apartment."

"I'll be fine," she assured him. "Go get some rest. We'll map out our strategy in the morning."

"That sounds fine. Good night, Angel."

Kyle made his way into the bedroom and closed the door behind him. Completely exhausted, he desperately needed to get some sleep. Tomorrow was already closing in on them. In a matter of hours, the sun would be up and Kyle was going to need all his strength in order to deal with whatever scenario awaited them.

Chapter Six

Kyle didn't sleep very well through the night. He tossed and turned repeatedly as he attempted to rest. He couldn't stop his mind from racing through the events of the evening. As a result of sleep deprivation, Kyle was irritated and not in a good mood. He also had some neck and lower back pain from all the tossing and turning he'd been doing throughout the night.

Only one day earlier, Kyle had closed a huge business deal with a new client. He'd actually been in really good spirits after landing that particular contract. His home-based computer business was finally showing some signs of life, in spite of a dreadful economy that had put the finishing touches on many local businesses in the upstate of South Carolina. But right now, Kyle's good mood was nowhere to be found. Then he remembered that Angel was in the living room, sleeping on the sofa. A bit of a smile returned to his face.

Kyle's watch was still working. It was a time piece that operated on a spring and had no internal, electronic components. According to the watch, it was about 7 o'clock in the morning. The sun was already shining brightly. The date was Saturday, December 22, 2012. Christmas was only three days away.

Kyle knocked on the bedroom door, giving Angel fair warning, before he made his way into the living room.

Angel was already up and seated on the sofa. She was wearing the same pair of blue jeans and yellow T-shirt from the previous night. She'd been reading the December issue of Time Magazine that Kyle had left on the floor, alongside the recliner. On the magazine cover was a big picture of Earth. In bright red letters, the date, *December 21, 2012,* was plastered across the page. A huge question mark had been printed squarely on the picture.

Angel looked up from the magazine as Kyle made his way into the room. She casually closed the publication and tossed it on the sofa. "I hope you don't mind," she said pausing for a moment. "I couldn't sleep any longer and needed something to read."

Kyle waved at her. "It's okay. I told you to make yourself at home."

"The power's still out," she informed him. "I checked the lights several times throughout the night. At least the sun's up. I blew out the candles after we went to bed. I thought, maybe, we should use them sparingly. We might need candles tonight."

"Good thinking," Kyle said. "Are you hungry? Did you snack on anything in the kitchen?"

Angel stood up from the sofa and stretched her arms towards the ceiling. "I had a banana and a package of trail mix. You'd better eat something, too. We don't know if any stores will be open today."

Kyle walked into the kitchen and grabbed some bottled water and a package of trail mix. They were quite fortunate that he'd purchased several boxes of packaged fruit from Sam's Club, a few days earlier. They could survive, if necessary, on the fruit and bottled water for a long time.

Angel walked into the kitchen area to confront Kyle. "What's our plan of attack?"

He smiled and finished drinking the bottled water he'd opened. "I think we need to see what's going on in the apartment complex, first. Then we need to find out if there's any news about what happened last night."

The two of them straightened out the apartment and got some blankets set up for later that evening. After stuffing their pockets with packages of trail mix, they headed outside and walked over to the parking lot.

Once they reached the parking lot, they could see that very few people were outside walking around. The two of them, slowly, made their way up to the front of the property where the rental office was located.

On the lower level of the building was the laundry facility. They walked inside the empty room. No machines were running. A few front loader washers still had clothes in them. They must have been in mid cycle when the power outage occurred. The owners of the clothes had, obviously, not taken the time to collect their belongings.

"Let's check out the rental office, upstairs," Kyle said. They walked over to the building's front entranceway. An impressive looking oak door greeted them. It was the very place where Kyle and Angel had first bumped into one another several days earlier. When Kyle tried the door handle, it was unlocked. He opened the door and they entered the rental office.

"Anyone home?" he yelled out.

"In here," a woman's voice echoed from an office that was situated off to their left. A short, slightly overweight, woman, with red, disheveled hair, poked her head out from behind the door. The woman, somewhat attractive looking, was dressed in a mauve colored sweat suit that was a few sizes too small for her. She'd applied some makeup to her face however; it looked like she'd done so in the dark.

"Good morning!" Kyle said. He'd, previously, interacted with the woman on a few occasions when paying the rent. He guessed that she was probably in her mid fifties. "I'm Kyle Wilson. I live in apartment F-15."

"Good morning, Kyle. Nice to see you again," the woman replied. "I'm Annie Hendricks." She walked over and shook his hand. "I'm the senior leasing manager."

"I'm Angel McClure." The assistant English professor extended her hand.

Annie shook Angel's hand. "Nice to see you again, as well, Ms. McClure." Annie had remembered Angel from when she'd visited the office to sign her apartment lease. "I'd offer the two of you some hot coffee and doughnuts but we don't have either of those luxuries in the office this morning with the power being out and all."

"What's the word on the street about the power outage?" Kyle asked.

Annie held up her two arms. She wore a frown across her face. "That's just the thing," she began, "there's no word on the street. I don't know if there's power in the surrounding areas, but I can tell you, for certain, that this complex is completely dead."

"How'd you get to work this morning?" Angel asked.

"I live on the premises," Annie replied. "All the other employees that work in this office live off property, in other communities. None of them have made it into work yet."

"Do you have phone service?" Kyle inquired.

"No. All the phones are dead. Even my mobile is fried. I can't get it to power up." Annie flipped open her BlackBerry and gave them a quick demonstration on how useless the device was.

Kyle moved over to the other side of the office so that he could look out a window to view the parking lot. As he gazed downward, he noticed a few residents were attempting to start their vehicles. From the looks of things, it didn't appear as if any of them were having much success. "Annie, have you tried to start your car yet?" Kyle asked.

Annie picked up a set of keys from her desktop and jingled them in her hand a few times before dropping them. "My car's dead, too. That was one of the first things I checked when I got up this morning."

"We didn't try to start our cars yet," Angel said. "We should really check to see if they're working, Kyle."

"I have a strong feeling that automobiles aren't going to work," Kyle replied. He continued to stare out the window at the parking lot. "But you're right, Angel. We should walk back to our building and check the cars to be absolutely certain."

"Listen, if you kids hear any news about what's going on, I'd really appreciate it if you'd be kind enough to share the information with me. I live in A-64 and I'll either be at this office or at my apartment, later this evening." Annie handed Angel a business card that contained her contact information.

Angel picked up a pencil she'd spotted on the Maplewood desk that was situated in the center of the small cream colored office. She proceeded to write down Annie's apartment number on the business card. "We'll certainly attempt to keep you in the loop about any information we uncover," Angel said as she carefully placed the card in the right front pocket of her blue jeans.

Kyle and Angel left the rental office and walked back to their apartment building so that they could attempt to start their cars.

Chapter Seven

Kyle turned the ignition key to start his red, 2011, Toyota Corolla. The car demonstrated absolutely no signs of life whatsoever. He turned the key again, and again, and then one final time. The car didn't make a sound. This, pretty much, confirmed what Kyle had feared all along. He believed the bright flash of light, that appeared the previous evening, had fried the electronic components in the vehicles within the immediate area. He didn't know if the incident was the result of a terrorist attack or from an unexplained natural event. They'd probably find out the answer to that question soon enough.

"This is a complete waste of time. The car's not going to start," he said as he looked up at Angel from inside the vehicle. She'd been positioned in front of the Corolla and had her ear pressed against the vehicle's hood listening for any sounds that might have been made from the engine.

"We had to give it a try," Angel said. She walked over to the car's driver side and leaned over to look at Kyle. "I want to check my car, too."

"It's not going to start," he explained to her.

"I have an older car. It might not have as many electronic gadgets as yours."

"What kind of car do you have?"

"A 73 Chevy Chevelle."

"That's not a car," he joked. "That's an antique!"

Kyle thought, for a moment, that perhaps Angel had a valid point. Maybe the old Chevy would run. He wasn't much of a mechanic, but he'd figured that a vehicle that old would certainly have very few electrical parts under the hood. *Hell,* he thought to himself, *it was worth a try*. Kyle smiled at her. "Let's go try to start your car."

When they reached Angel's Chevy, Kyle was shocked to see that the vehicle was in mint condition. She'd taken very good care of her automobile. It was painted a light shade of yellow. Kyle guessed that the car was probably worth a lot of money to some collectors.

"How long have you had this car?" he asked.

"I purchased it two years ago from a friend who lives in Indiana," she replied.

Angel opened the car's door and climbed into the driver seat. The interior was made of black vinyl fabric.

She sat there a moment before turning towards Kyle. "What are you waiting for?"

"What do you mean?" Kyle replied.

"Aren't you going to get in the car?"

Kyle grinned. "It's not going to start, Angel."

"Just get in the car," she insisted.

Kyle chuckled, slowly walked around to the passenger side, and opened the door. After he climbed in and shut the door, he looked over at her and started laughing. "Are you going to start this thing or are we just going to sit here the entire morning?"

"Fasten your seatbelt," she told him. She was also laughing at this point. "Don't you know the state of South Carolina has a seatbelt law – *Click It or Ticket!*

"Angel, I seriously doubt that you're going to get your car started. And if by some miracle, on Earth, you do get it to run, I don't think the state police are going to be overly concerned, today, about *Click It or...* " Before Kyle could finish his sentence, Angel started her Chevy. It turned over on the very first try.

Kyle was shocked. He really hadn't expected the car to start. "Well I'll be damned," he said with a bit of surprise apparent in his voice.

"And you were saying?" she asked in a mildly sarcastic tone.

"I was saying that it's a damn good thing you reminded me to wear my seatbelt."

Chapter Eight

Angel, gently, pulled down on the gear shift and locked the car into drive. Very slow, she drove the 73 Chevy through the apartment complex parking lot. A few residents, congregating outside, stared at them as they passed by. No doubt they were wondering how the twosome had been able to get the car to run.

Kyle noticed that Angel's Chevy had nearly a full tank of gas. *That was a good thing*, he thought to himself. He figured that it was going to be difficult for them to get additional fuel with the current power outage affecting the community and possibly some surrounding cities. In a worst case scenario, they'd probably be forced to siphon gas from other cars if service stations weren't open.

"I want to check the traffic flow on the local highways," Angel said as she pulled away from the property's main entranceway. She turned the Chevy onto a public access road that tied into the highway. The two of them looked for signs of traffic, but no one else seemed to be on the road.

"I think we have the highway to ourselves," Kyle said.

Angel was driving at about 35 miles per hour. As they made their way down the road, they spotted a car coming from the opposite direction. Angel immediately reduced the Chevy's speed as they approached the oncoming automobile. When they got a little closer, Kyle and Angel realized the other vehicle, a red Taurus, was not actually moving. It had been abandoned on the road. Angel stopped the Chevy in order to let Kyle get out and assess the situation.

"Keep the car running," he told her as he walked away from the Chevy and approached the Taurus. He moved towards the abandoned car with a bit of caution. Once he observed the scene was safe, and no one was around; Kyle peered inside the driver side window. Upon his further inspection, he saw that the vehicle appeared to be in perfectly good condition. He could also see that the keys had been removed from the ignition.

"What are you looking for?" Angel asked him.

"Nothing in particular," he replied. Kyle walked around the vehicle and gazed momentarily at the small door compartment that protected the car's gas cap. He reached down, to the ground, and picked up a medium size rock he'd spotted. He proceeded to bang the rock up against the gas cap door.

"What are you doing?" Angel yelled at him.

Kyle ignored her question and continued striking the plastic door with the rock. After several sharp blows, the plastic door cracked and fell to the ground leaving the gas cap exposed. Kyle examined the gas cap for a moment, walked back to the Chevy, and climbed into the passenger seat.

"What the hell was that all about?" Angel asked.

"Sooner or later we're going to need some gas for your car. I seriously doubt if we'll be able to buy any fuel from a service station. I was just trying to figure out a safe way to be able to access some *regular unleaded* for the future. I think I've solved the problem."

Angel nodded as she listened to Kyle's explanation. She, suddenly, realized that the Chevy wouldn't run, indefinitely, on its current tank of gas.

Angel pulled away from the Taurus and continued driving down the road. After proceeding a few hundred yards, they came upon another car that had been abandoned on the road. This time it was a green Volkswagen and the car was positioned in their driving lane. Angel carefully swerved around the green bug, and they could plainly see that no one was inside the vehicle. As they continued to drive farther down the highway, Kyle and Angel observed many abandoned vehicles that had been stranded on or alongside the highway.

"This is so strange," Kyle said. He pondered the possibility that Angel's Chevy was the only vehicle operating within the entire county.

After driving for several more miles, they turned into a Li'l Cricket convenience store. One other car, a gold Kia Spectra, was parked outside the store's parking lot.

Kyle exited the Chevy and leaned back inside the car to speak to Angel. "Keep the engine running and the doors locked. I'm going to see if anyone's inside."

"I want to come inside too," Angel complained.

"It might not be safe. I'd feel a lot better if you'd stay here. If we do have the only car in the area that's working, someone inside the store might want to take it off our hands."

"Okay," she replied with just a trace of disappointment detectable in her voice. In reality, she understood the logic of Kyle's request. She turned around and locked both car doors.

Angel watched Kyle as he approached the Li'l Cricket store and eventually walked inside the building. About five minutes passed, and there was still no sign of him. She began to grow anxious. Angel tried to look inside the store's front window but was unable to see anything from her position in the parking lot.

The sudden sound of gunshots completely startled her. There were three distinct blasts that occurred in rapid succession. She could tell that the gunfire had originated from inside the building. The next thing Angel saw was Kyle running, at top speed, away from the convenience store.

Chapter Nine

"Open the door!" Kyle yelled. He was running as fast as he could towards the Chevy.

Angel immediately reached over to open the passenger door. In the distance, she heard the sound of additional gunfire. Only a few yards separated Kyle and the car door. When he finally reached the Chevy, he quickly flung his body inside the car.

Angel didn't even wait for him to close the door. She had her right foot firmly pressed on the accelerator pedal. The yellow car spun its wheels against the loose stones on the store's gravel parking lot. Some stones got kicked up into the air and struck the storefront. The passenger door was swinging wildly back and forth as the Chevy's tires struggled to maintain traction with the parking lot. Angel finally managed to get the car under control as the vehicle's wheels made contact with the firmer surface of the highway. She made a sharp right turn and headed down the road, away from the convenience store.

Kyle finally managed to get the passenger door closed and proceeded to fasten his seatbelt.

"What in the hell happened back there?" Angel asked as she drove the car down the highway at 75 miles per hour.

Kyle glanced over his shoulder just to make sure that no one was following them. He'd forgotten that Angel's car seemed to be the only vehicle working in the entire county. "The store manager was absolutely crazy," he explained to her. "He thought we were terrorists. He kept on rambling about how we were trying to take over his country."

"You were in there for a really long time," Angel said.

"I asked the guy if he'd heard any news about what's happened. He said the local police came by his place earlier. Evidently, some local deputies rode up, on bicycles, and told him that terrorists were behind everything that's taken place. He said the sheriff's office believed the entire country had been attacked."

"A terrorist attack?" Angel said. She shook her head with skepticism. "Where are they? I don't see any terrorists running around here."

Kyle shrugged his shoulders. "I'm only telling you what that nut job, back there, said. He also wanted to know how we were able to get your car running. The police must've told him that all the cars, in the region, had been knocked out of commission by the terrorists."

"So that idiot thought we were terrorists because my car was working?" Angel said.

"Basically, yes."

Once again, Kyle turned around to look out the Chevy's back window. He could see that no one was following them. "I think you can slow down, Angel. We're in the clear."

Angel looked at the speedometer and lessened the pressure on the car's accelerator. The Chevy immediately began to respond and soon reached a much slower speed. "Why'd he start shooting at you?" Angel asked.

Kyle shook his head a few times from side to side. He was still in a mild state of shock. "He pulled a gun on me, from behind the counter, and said he wanted your car. The guy insisted on driving us to the police station in Spartanburg. I pushed over a shelf of food to try and knock the gun out of his hand. It actually worked, but the damn shelf blocked my exit from the store. He became really pissed off and picked up the gun and began shooting. I just started running, out of there, as fast as I could."

"You scared the hell out of me," Angel said.

"You should've been in the store," Kyle replied.

Just ahead, Angel saw another vehicle which had been abandoned on the road. She slowed the Chevy's speed down to a crawl and carefully maneuvered around the tan Volvo. As they passed by the car, something caught Kyle's attention.

"Angel, stop the car!" he yelled.

She slammed her foot on the brake pedal and the Chevy came to a sudden stop.

Chapter Ten

"What are you going to do with a garden hose?" Angel asked as she and Kyle peered through the Volvo's rear driver side window.

"We'll use it to siphon gas from other vehicles," he explained. Kyle tried to open the car's back door, but it was locked. He and Angel tried the other doors, but they were locked as well.

"Do you have anything, in the trunk, which we can use to break the window?"

"There should be a crowbar inside," Angel said.

Kyle snatched the car keys from inside the Chevy and opened the trunk. Sure enough, there was a crowbar in the trunk compartment. He grabbed the tool and proceeded to walk over to the Volvo.

"You might want to move away from the car," he warned her.

Angel backed away as Kyle started to pound the daylights out of the back driver side window. After a few swings with the crowbar, the safety glass cracked into hundreds of small pieces. Kyle was able to push through the tiny shards of glass with the tool. He reached inside the back seat and snatched the garden hose.

"You made that look pretty easy," Angel said. She'd noticed how resourceful Kyle was. Angel could see that he possessed good survival skills. No matter what type of situation they'd found themselves in, he seemed up to the challenge of finding a clever way to resolve the problem.

"This should work fine," Kyle said as he examined the hose. He walked over to the Chevy's trunk and tossed the crowbar and garden hose inside.

"Kyle, I think we should take a ride over to the USC Upstate campus. There might be some faculty members, in the science department, that can help us figure out what's happening around here."

Kyle closed the trunk and walked over to Angel. "That sounds like a really good idea. Maybe they've been in touch with the authorities or have some information from outside the state?"

They got back inside the car and headed towards the interstate. On the way over to the campus, Angel and Kyle encountered many abandoned vehicles on Interstate 85. A fair number of people were seated in their cars, but a lot of the automobiles they'd spotted had been abandoned without any signs of their owners being present.

Angel turned off I-85 at the USC Upstate exit and crossed over a small bridge that brought them onto the campus property. As they drove on the university roads, they saw a few students hanging around some college buildings and dormitories.

Angel pulled the Chevy into the faculty parking area. There were only four other cars parked in the entire lot.

The empty faculty parking lot made a lot of sense to Kyle. The brilliant flash of light had occurred on a Friday evening at around 9 o'clock. He figured that most faculty members had already vacated the campus by then. In addition, he knew the fall semester had recently concluded, for the upcoming Christmas holiday, and that most students and staff members wouldn't be returning until later in January.

"I think the car will be safe here," Angel said as she turned off the engine.

Kyle looked around the parking area and didn't see anyone nearby. "I think you're right, Angel."

"We should probably walk over to the campus security building. It's only about a hundred yards from here," Angel said.

When they reached the security building, Kyle and Angel were excited to find several campus officers present outside the complex. The officers had set up two, white plastic tables and some blue folding chairs in front of the two-story brick building.

Angel walked over to a security officer that had been seated behind one of two tables and held out her arm to shake his hand. "Hi, I'm Angel McClure. I teach in the English department. Can you please tell me what's happening?"

The security officer stood up and shook Angel's hand. The man was a husky, average looking fellow with dark brown hair and a gray colored beard. He had on a brown and gold security uniform. "Good morning Ma'am." The guard was obviously quite engrossed with Angel's good looks. He thoroughly eyed the assistant professor up and down several times. "My name's Keith Tanner. Right now, the only information I have is from the local authorities. I know that the power's out throughout the county. There aren't too many automobiles working, either. We've had no phones or radios since last night."

"Did the authorities happen to mention what might have caused all these problems?" Kyle asked.

The officer turned to face him. "According to some local fellows, there's a rumor that our country's been attacked by Arab terrorists."

"Can you tell me where the closest police department is located?" Kyle asked.

"We have a small county sheriff's office right on campus," the security guard replied. "You know, we've been in and out of contact with a few local police departments ever since everything began to get crazy last night."

"Have you been in touch with any other counties in the upstate?" Angel asked.

"I don't know about other counties? There are some deputies patrolling around on bicycles. They've been checking some things out. We're still waiting for some of those guys to return. Hopefully, they'll be able to tell us how many Arabs are running around out there."

Angel rolled her eyes in response to the security guard's comment about the Arabs.

Kyle started laughing.

"I'd really like to check out the science department. Maybe a faculty doctor is on campus," Angel said to Kyle.

"I just came from the science building and nobody's over there," Keith replied. "I don't believe that any faculty members are here today. That is except for you, Ms. McClure." Keith was grinning broadly at Angel.

Just then, a deputy rode up on a red mountain bicycle. The man was dressed in a dark colored windbreaker that had the words "SHERRIF'S OFFICE" printed on it in bright yellow letters. The deputy was tall and handsome. He had an athletic looking build with closely cropped black hair and a finely manicured moustache.

"Hey David, what's going on?" the campus guard said to the deputy.

"Hi, Keith," the deputy replied. "We just received some pretty interesting news about 20 minutes ago." The officer was slightly out of breath.

"What kind of news?" Keith asked.

The deputy eyed Kyle and Angel as he parked his bike alongside one of the white tables. "Some deputies made an important discovery about 30 miles outside of downtown Spartanburg. We're going to conduct a press conference, in the Hodge Center, at noon. You'll definitely want to attend that conference."

Chapter Eleven

The Hodge Center was a 1,535-seat multi-purpose arena located in the middle of the USC Upstate campus. The building was normally home to the university's Spartan basketball team. Today, it was to be the official location for an important press conference that was being held by the Spartanburg County Sheriff's Office.

It was a few minutes after 1 o'clock before the sheriff's office finally began the noon press conference. Kyle thought it was odd that the deputies, in charge, referred to the event as a press conference since no members of the press were actually present at the Hodge Center.

Kyle and Angel were pleasantly surprised to find some lights shining brightly in the classroom they were using as the conference room. The sheriff's office had managed to find several gasoline generators that were operational. It was somewhat comforting to Kyle and Angel to see the lights working. There was even a microphone set up on a small platform in the front of the conference room. It had been successfully connected to the speaker system that was hardwired into the building.

Kyle spotted a couple of empty seats that were located in the last row of chairs, in the very back of the room. Kyle estimated that there were about a hundred people, made up mostly of resident students, at the press conference.

Shortly after they had taken their seats, a deputy, dressed in a dark blue uniform, slowly made his way up to the platform where the microphone was positioned. The deputy was a short fellow with sandy colored hair and a blond moustache. He tapped on the microphone several times with his finger to make sure the device was working properly.

"Testing, one, two, three," he spoke into the microphone. "Can you hear me okay?"

A few people in the crowd yelled back that the volume and clarity of his voice were perfect.

"Good afternoon," he began. "Let me preface my remarks by stating that the information I am about to read is considered reliable. I have been in recent contact with various deputies within the sheriff's office. We have been able to confirm the following information from multiple law enforcement sources.

"In the past several hours, we have restored the working capability of some of our communication instruments. Most equipment, which is currently operational, consists of two-way radios. This, in itself, is a significant development because it will allow the sheriff's office to greatly improve the speed and accuracy of gathering and reporting important information to law enforcement departments and civilians. Up until a few hours ago, we had been relying, solely, on deputies riding bicycles to deliver information to various command centers.

"We are going to attempt to deliver updated information, to civilians, approximately every three hours, right in this room. If there are no significant updates to report, we will post a sign, on the front door of this building, indicating that fact. Updated information will also be reported at the other sheriff's office locations throughout Spartanburg County."

"What's happening throughout the rest of the county?" a young black girl, in blue jeans and a green shirt, asked. She'd been standing against a wall, near the back of the room, not too far away from Kyle and Angel. "I've heard some rumors that the police department has news about terrorists in the area."

The crowd became a bit restless as multiple people began asking questions at the same time.

The deputy put his hands up in the air, signaling the audience to be quiet. "I do have some updated information to pass along. If everyone refrains from attempting to speak out at the same time, it will be easier for me to discuss the information that I have been given." The deputy waited for the audience to settle down. "We have been able to make contact with local law enforcement authorities in about a 30 mile radius from downtown Spartanburg. The contacts we have established are all reporting very similar conditions to what we have experienced. Within that 30 mile radius, there are visible signs of people and normal infrastructure. For the most part, motor vehicles are not working. Some older model cars have been observed operating on a few county roads." The deputy paused for a moment to drink some bottled water that had been placed on the lectern he'd been reading from. "The most troubling news I have to report has to do with our continued inability to make contact with anyone outside the 30 mile radius I spoke about."

"What exactly does that mean?" asked a heavyset guy wearing a red shirt with white stripes in the front row. The man had wire-rimmed glasses and looked as if he'd been awake since the previous night. His eyes were bloodshot and closely matched the color of his shirt.

The deputy straightened his posture and readjusted the microphone stand accordingly. "We don't know, at this point, what any of this means. We are trying to reestablish contact with authorities in surrounding counties. As soon as we have successfully reestablished those contacts, we will be sure to update civilians. As far as the rumors regarding terrorists, they remain just that—rumors. There have been no confirmed reports of any terrorist activities in Spartanburg County. That's all I have to report to you at this time. The next update is scheduled to take place at 3 o'clock this afternoon, in this room."

A significant number of people rushed the deputy as he attempted to leave the small platform. The crowd of people obviously wanted further clarification about what was taking place within the county.

Kyle and Angel left the conference area from an exit that was situated near the back of the room. Kyle was leading the way. He walked swiftly, his pace quickening with each step. Angel followed slightly behind him. She could tell that he was headed towards the security building again.

"Slow down," Angel said as she tried to keep up with him. "Where's the fire?"

"I want to talk with that deputy named David. He knows something about what's going on."

"Don't you think the other deputy, pretty much, covered everything during the press conference?" Angel asked.

"No," Kyle said. "I think they're doing what all forms of government usually do in these situations."

"What's that?" Angel said as she walked briskly across the campus still trying to match steps with him.

"They're holding back important information. They don't want people to panic, so they conveniently leave out important details. The only problem with that practice is that the details they're leaving out might be important to our continued survival."

They finally reached the security building where the campus guards were still seated behind the two tables they'd set up. The heavyset guard named Keith Tanner was there along with two other campus guards that they'd observed earlier.

"Hi Keith," Kyle called out.

The guard stood up from behind the table and shook his hand. "Did you guys just come from the Hodge Center?" he asked.

"Yes," Kyle replied. "Have you seen that deputy who was here earlier? The one on the bicycle, named David?"

"He just left about five minutes ago," Keith said.

"Dammit!" Kyle was disgusted he'd missed the lawman.

"Maybe I can help you," said another security guard who had been seated behind one of the tables. The tall skinny guard stood up and approached Kyle. The man had a poor complexion with a lot of acne visible on his face and neck.

Kyle wiped away the perspiration from the top of his forehead. Even though it was only a few days before Christmas, the temperature in the Upstate of South Carolina was in the lower 70's and the humidity had been pretty high. "I just wanted to get some clarification on what that deputy, David, was talking about. He had mentioned something about a discovery that was made outside of Spartanburg County. He spoke as though the deputies were going to discuss the topic during the press conference, but it never came up."

"My name is Sam," the guard said as he shook Kyle's hand.

"Hi, Sam. My name is Kyle Wilson."

"Kyle, I think that there's a lot of confusion going on. The sheriff's office has a lot of deputies, riding around on bicycles, gathering information and trying to sort this situation out so that we can report accurate details to civilians. A lot of people are jumping to conclusions that are, in some instances, probably not reflective of what's really happening. I'm not sure what David meant about a discovery outside of Spartanburg County, but I'm confident that the sheriff's office will keep us updated about important information as they piece everything together."

Kyle was incensed by Sam's response. He knew that the campus security guard was holding back important information, but he didn't want to burn the bridge of communication they'd already established.

"You're right, Sam. We'll just wait to hear the updates from the deputies at the scheduled press conferences. Thanks for your help." Kyle walked away from the security guard and Angel followed closely behind him.

"Where are we heading now?" Angel asked.

"We're heading back to your car," he replied. "I've got a plan."

Chapter Twelve

When Kyle and Angel reached the Chevy it was nearly two o'clock in the afternoon. The sun was still shining brightly in the Carolina sky.

They noticed an older, blue pickup truck had parked alongside of Angel's car. The vehicle had not been there when they arrived earlier in the day. It was a beat up old Ford. On the back bumper was a USC Upstate faculty parking decal. On the tailgate was a green, faded bumper sticker that read:

| I LOVE PHYSICS, |
| BUT GRAVITY GETS ME DOWN! |

Kyle and Angel looked at each other. They were thinking the same thing. "We have to check the science building." The words came out of their mouths at, practically, the same time.

It was only a short walk to the Horace C. Smith Science Building. When they arrived, the facility was open and the two of them were able to walk right inside. The interior of the building was pretty dark without the presence of any lighting. Angel and Kyle walked down a short corridor and made a quick left turn. They heard a noise at the far end of the hallway.

"Hello," Angel yelled out. There was no reply.

They continued to walk down the hallway and heard another noise followed by, what sounded like, someone tapping something with a hammer.

"Hello, is anyone here?" Angel yelled out again. Suddenly, the tapping noise stopped. A silhouette of a person appeared at the very end of a long corridor. It was too dark to make out the individual's features.

"I haven't had a chance to post the final grades yet," a voice said. "With the power outage, you're going to have to wait until next week."

"We're not students. My name is Angel McClure and I'm a faculty member in the English department. This is my friend, Kyle Wilson. We wanted to speak with a faculty member from the science department."

There was a slight pause.

"Oh," the man said. "In that case, come on down to my office. I've got a battery rigged up that's powering a light."

They proceeded to walk in the direction of the man's office. They'd both noticed the strong and unmistakable aroma of laboratory chemicals that had been present throughout the building. Kyle had, vaguely, remembered that the science labs were somewhere nearby. As a former student and employee at the university, he'd only been in the science building on a couple of occasions. The computer science and IT departments, the locations he'd frequented as a student and an employee at the university, were located at an alternate facility, away from the main campus.

When they got to the end of the hallway, they spotted a dim light escaping through the cracks of a partially opened door.

"Hi, I'm Dr. Paul Grossman," said a short elderly man standing alongside the door. "I'm the director and senior professor within the physics department here at the university. Come inside my office where we can see one another."

The three of them went into the professor's office. Kyle noticed that the man was a pleasant looking fellow, probably in his early to mid sixties. He had, what looked like, a healthy tan, thinned out gray hair, and a magnificent looking complexion for his age. The professor was wearing black-framed glasses. They were the type of glasses that Kyle imagined a professor of physics would wear.

"What can I do for you two young people?" The professor stared intently at Kyle, studying the finely chiseled features of his handsome face.

"We were hoping to cross paths with someone from the science department to see if they could shed some light on what's been happening here in the upstate," Angel said.

"Oh, I see," the professor replied. He took off his glasses and wiped the lenses gently with a paper towel that he'd picked up from a brown metal desk that was situated in the center of his office.

Kyle noticed that the professor's office was a tiny cubby hole, stuffed with papers and notebooks. In the room's right corner were three tan filing cabinets that looked like they'd seen better days. A small circular fan was positioned on top of the middle filing cabinet. From the looks of it, Kyle guessed the fan might have been the first one ever invented. On the other side of the office was an old chalkboard and it was filled up with mathematical formulas that had been scribbled in different directions. Kyle couldn't figure out what was more disorganized, the blackboard filled with chalk or the office clutter. He decided it was too close to call.

"Well, my young friends, I fear that something very bad has happened." The professor inspected the glasses he'd just cleaned and repositioned them back over his eyes.

"That's the reason why we wanted to talk with you," Angel said. "We just came from a press conference that was held by the sheriff's office and the deputy, running the presentation, was very vague about what's been going on. We walked away feeling like the authorities were deliberately attempting to hide something."

The professor sat down on an old orange chair. It had more cracks in it than actual material. "What did the deputy tell you?"

"Pretty much, what we already know," Angel said. "He explained that the power was out across the entire county and that very few automobiles were running."

"Did he mention anything about the surrounding counties?"

Kyle stared intently at the professor. He could tell the older man was really sharp and that he probably had his own ideas about what had taken place. He entered the conversation. "The deputy did make a comment that the sheriff's office had not been able to communicate with anyone outside of a thirty mile radius from the center of Spartanburg."

Professor Grossman had his hands clasped behind the back of his head. "Do you youngsters live near the campus?" he asked.

We live in an apartment complex about ten miles from here," Angel replied.

"How'd you get here, today?"

"For some reason, my 73 Chevy still runs."

The professor smiled as he continued to study their faces. "The older vehicles, without the fancy electronics, seem to work quite well. I have an old Ford pickup and it started right up."

"Yeah, we know," Kyle said. "You parked next to Angel's car."

"That yellow Chevy, in the parking lot, is your car? Nice set of wheels you have there, Angel. You've kept the vehicle in excellent condition."

"Dr. Grossman, would you consider helping us find out what the hell is going on around here?" Kyle asked.

The professor smiled. "I'm a man of science. My entire life I have always loved the challenge of explaining things through the application of very logical equations. What has happened to us defies logic at first glance. But I believe there's a logical explanation for everything that occurs. Sometimes we have to look a little harder or dig a bit deeper, but sooner or later the logical explanation will reveal itself.

"I would love to help the two of you get to the bottom of this mystery. What do you want me to do? I'm a college professor. How can I possibly help you?"

"Dr. Grossman, I'd really like to..."

"Please call me Paul," the professor interrupted Kyle. "When people call me doctor, it makes me feel so much older."

Kyle laughed. "Alright Paul, I have a plan that I'd like you to hear. I want to drive Angel's Chevy out past the 30 mile zone that the deputies spoke about. I want to see, for myself, what's really going on out there."

Angel looked at Kyle. She suddenly had a worried look etched across her face. "Kyle, we never discussed driving out there."

Kyle turned towards Angel. "I know I hadn't mentioned this earlier. I was going to tell you when we got back to the car." He wheeled around to look at the professor. "I was going to explain it to her, Paul, but when we got to the faculty parking lot; we spotted your truck and decided to come over here to the science building." He shifted around again to look at Angel. "I'm sorry I didn't discuss it with you, first."

"I don't know, Kyle, suppose it's not safe?"

"It'll be safe." He moved closer to her. "Look, Angel, your car operates without any problems and it has plenty of gas to get us out there and back again safely. I promise you we'll be careful."

Angel looked at the professor. "I want Paul to come with us. He might be able to help."

"Then you're okay with us driving the car?" Kyle asked.

Angel nodded. "I still don't think it's safe, but I'll go along with your idea if you think it's, absolutely, necessary."

The professor was grinning as he looked at Kyle and Angel. "When do we leave?"

Angel eyed the professor. "If we're going to do this, I think we should wait until tomorrow morning. It's getting way too late, in the day, to drive out there now. We need to take food and water to be safe. We don't know what we're going to encounter and we also need to allow ourselves enough daylight to drive the entire sixty miles."

"I agree with Angel," the professor said. "We should prepare this evening and leave first thing in the morning."

"That's fine with me," Kyle replied as he looked at his watch. It was approaching three o'clock. "Angel, we should begin heading back to the apartment. We promised Annie that we'd fill her in on what's happening. We also need to find something to eat. I'm getting hungry."

Paul reached under his desk and picked up an unopened package of Oreo cookies. He tossed them to Kyle. "Eat up my boy. I've got more junk food hidden in this office than anything else," he joked.

"Thanks," Kyle said.

"Paul, where would you like for us to meet you in the morning?" Angel asked.

"Meet me at the Hodge Center a few minutes before 9 o'clock. There's another press conference scheduled tomorrow morning at the top of the hour. We should listen to what the deputies have to say. We can get on the road after the conference."

"We'll see you tomorrow morning," Kyle said. They shook the professor's hand and headed back to the faculty parking lot.

Chapter Thirteen

On the way back to the apartment, Kyle and Angel broke open the large package of Oreos. After they started to eat the cream filled cookies, they both realized how hungry they'd been. They couldn't swallow them fast enough.

"I don't normally eat junk food," Kyle said as he stuffed his face with another cookie.

"Me either," Angel replied. She reached over and plucked out two more for herself.

Kyle looked over at Angel and said, "I have some frozen hamburgers in the freezer. They're probably almost defrosted by now. I was thinking that we should barbecue those babies outside the back of my apartment when we get home. I'd hate for all that good meat to spoil."

Angel nodded. "You'll need a grill and some charcoal."

"I have all that and lots of matches. You know what else?"

"What?" Angel laughed.

I have hamburger rolls, pickles, and potato chips."

"That sounds like a slice of heaven," Angel said.

Angel pulled into the apartment complex at three forty-five in the afternoon. She parked the Chevy right in front of the rental office. They wanted to check on Annie and invite her to the apartment for dinner. Before they could unfasten their seatbelts, Annie Hendricks walked outside the rental office. She'd spotted Angel's Chevy as they pulled up to the office.

"I see that one of your cars is still working," she yelled out to them. Annie walked up to the passenger side where Kyle was seated.

"Would you like some Oreos?" Kyle asked her as he held up the package of cookies.

Annie smiled. "If you don't mind, I think I'll take you up on your offer, Mr. Wilson." Annie reached over and pulled out a few cookies.

"Annie, please take some more," Kyle encouraged her.

She smiled and reached back into the package and grabbed three more cookies. "Thanks! I am pretty hungry."

"By the way, Annie, we're going to cook some burgers on my grill tonight. I have a lot of hamburger meat that is still good. If we don't use it by tonight, it's going to go bad. Angel and I would really like for you to

73

come over and join us for dinner. Besides, we need to fill you in on everything that we learned today. You can tell us what's happened around here as well. What do you say? Will you join us?"

A big smile appeared on Annie's face. "You guys are so sweet. As long as you don't mind, I'm not going to turn away a free meal and some companionship."

"Great!" Angel said.

"I'm sure you already know my apartment number," Kyle chuckled. "Just in case you forgot it, it's F-15. Come on over in about an hour."

"It's a date," Annie said. She gave them a quick wave and walked back up the sidewalk and into the rental office.

A few minutes later, Kyle and Angel entered the apartment. Everything appeared just the way they'd left it, earlier in the day. Kyle had been slightly worried that vandals might have tried to enter the premises. With the power outage in effect and the police unable to respond to emergencies, he knew that opportunists would be out in full force. Fortunately, they'd spared his place on this particular day.

Kyle opened the freezer and found the hamburger patties, pretty well, defrosted. He scooped them up and placed them on a large white dish.

In the dining room, Angel set the oak colored table with paper dinner plates, plastic utensils, and some old birthday napkins that she'd found in the kitchen drawers.

"I'm going to start cooking these patties," Kyle said. He placed some charcoal pieces in the bottom of a small black grill that was on the back patio and dropped a lighted match onto the charcoal. He gave the grill a few squirts of lighter fluid and watched as the flames grew in intensity.

It didn't take very long for the smell of cooking hamburger meat to start permeating the air.

"My goodness, that smells awesome," Angel said.

"That it does," Kyle agreed. He flipped over the burgers, one by one, as he tried to cook the meat evenly on both sides.

Just then, Annie knocked on the door. Angel greeted her. She'd brought over a box of chocolate doughnuts for dessert.

"Oh Annie, that's going to put the finishing touches on a wonderful dinner."

"Annie, have a seat on the sofa and make yourself at home," Kyle yelled from the back porch.

Annie sat down on the sofa and Angel joined her after she put the doughnuts on the dining room table. "Did anything unusual happen around here today?" Angel asked.

"No one made it into work this morning. We usually work a full day on Saturdays, but I was all alone the entire day."

"You didn't really expect the staff to show up, did you?"

"No, I guess not. By the way, there were some nasty fights that broke out in the parking lot near the rental office after the two of you left this morning. It was pretty scary. I didn't know what to do. It's not like I could call the police or anything."

"What happened?" Kyle asked as he walked into the apartment with a large plate of cooked burgers.

"After awhile, the yelling and fighting stopped. The mob in the parking lot finally dispersed."

"People are just wound up," Angel said. "This is a very stressful time. You have to expect that kind of behavior. We'll have to be extra careful when we're around large crowds."

"Let's eat!" Kyle said.

The three of them sat at the dining room table and feasted on the burgers, pickles, and chips. It wasn't the fanciest of dinners, but it was absolutely delicious and quite filling at the same time.

They exchanged stories about what had transpired throughout the day. Angel told Annie about how Kyle had been shot at by the Li'l Cricket store manager, and how many abandoned cars they'd encountered on the highways. Kyle filled in Annie on what had occurred at the university and how they'd met the physicist, Dr. Paul Grossman. He explained to Annie about their plans to drive to the outer limits of Spartanburg County, the next morning, and how the sheriff's office had been unable to establish contact with civilians or law enforcement officials beyond a distance of 30 miles in all directions. Kyle invited Annie to go with them in the morning. Annie instantly accepted his offer.

For dessert, they snacked on the chocolate doughnuts that Annie had brought over. Kyle had eaten more junk food in one day than he'd consumed the entire year. But for some strange reason, he didn't really care about junk food or anything else. Maybe he was in such a carefree mood because he was having such a great time and because he knew that there were no cell phones, computers, televisions or any other forms of technology that could interrupt this night. The regular daily distractions, otherwise known as modern technology, which had been so important in all of their lives, were gone. Kyle was enjoying the food, the company of his two new friends, and the fact that he was alive to take it all in.

Chapter Fourteen

Later that evening, Kyle and Angel rested quietly in the apartment. Kyle sat on the recliner and Angel on the brown leather sofa. The candles were already burning brightly throughout the apartment. It was quite warm in the room without the air conditioner running. Angel was wearing a red USC T-Shirt and some white shorts she'd retrieved from her apartment while Kyle had on a pair of red shorts and a white tank top.

"Angel, how long have you been teaching English," Kyle asked as he finished reading the Time Magazine article titled, *December 21, 2012?*

"I've been teaching for seven years," she replied. Angel had been staring at the apartment ceiling. Not focusing on anything in particular, she'd been casually observing the random arrangement of white popcorn flakes that adhered to the ceiling's surface. She'd wondered if her introduction to Kyle had been an act of randomness or some sort of Divine Intervention to help her survive the current crisis.

"Do you enjoy teaching your students?"

Angel thought about Kyle's question for a moment before answering. "Yes, I really do. I enjoy working with them. It gives me a sense of satisfaction when I'm able to explain concepts to others and help people to become better communicators."

"You're really lucky, Angel."

"Why do you say that?" she asked him.

Kyle dropped the Time Magazine on the floor and turned, slightly, to face her. "Think about how many people in the world go to a job every single day, and hate that they have to do so. Imagine how awful it must be to spend your life working for a certain company and you don't enjoy being there. You're lucky because you enjoy teaching your students."

"Yeah, I don't ever think of teaching as a job. USC has been a wonderful place to instruct. I can't speak for the Upstate campus because I haven't taught a class there yet, but I'm confident that they'll treat me well."

"I'm sure they'll love you," Kyle said.

"Kyle, what service do you offer in your computer business?"

Kyle shifted his body again in the recliner. "I build websites for small businesses."

"Is it very difficult to build a website?" she wanted to know.

"Not if you know how to do it," he said jokingly.

"Very funny," she said as she rolled her eyes at his sarcastic answer. Angel picked up the bottled water that had been resting on the tan carpet and took a sip from it. "Kyle, aren't you concerned about what we might discover tomorrow?"

Kyle's facial expression took on a more serious appearance. "I'd be lying to you if I said that I wasn't concerned. In all honesty, I'm kind of excited to find out what the heck is going on. I'm a big fan of dealing with reality. Regardless of what we discover, bad or good, I think it's better to know the truth. Once we know what we're dealing with, we'll learn how to adapt to the situation. That's what life's all about, Angel. You either adapt to the environment you're living in or you die."

"Boy, I didn't realize that you were such a deep thinker, Kyle Wilson." Angel stood up and walked into the kitchen to get some more bottled water. "Do you want anything while I'm in here?"

"No, I'm fine," he said.

It had been a long and eventful day for the both of them and tomorrow would, no doubt, bring its own set of challenges they'd have to contend with.

Kyle and Angel were pretty exhausted and looked forward to getting some rest. Kyle had decided that he'd sleep in the bedroom, again, and Angel would spend the night on the sofa.

"Good night," Kyle said as he walked over to Angel.

"Good night, Kyle," she replied.

For a second, they turned and stared at each other, their eyes taking in the awkwardness of the moment. Kyle started to turn away, but before he could, Angel gently wrapped her arms around his body and gave him a light kiss on the lips. "Thanks for taking me in when I was too afraid to be alone, and thanks for being an all-around great guy."

Kyle did everything humanly possible to maintain his composure. He really wanted to spend the night with Angel but knew that now wasn't the right time for him to act on his emotions. He smiled at her. "You're welcome, Angel. Don't worry; everything is going to turn out okay."

Chapter Fifteen

Kyle had been dreaming about a computer project. He kept attempting to use a specific jpeg image for a particular web design, but the file just refused to upload onto the template he'd selected. In his dream, Kyle was so frustrated by the incompatible image file; he began pounding his fists repeatedly on the computer desk in front of him. The sound of his hands, striking the desk, was so loud that it woke him from a deep sleep.

Wide awake, he realized that something was terribly wrong. He still heard the pounding noise, only Kyle wasn't dreaming.

"Angel!" he yelled out loud as he rolled onto his right side, and sprang off the king size sleigh bed. Just as he'd practiced many times before, in his mind's eye, he slid open the small drawer of the walnut constructed night dresser, situated on the side of his bed, and placed his right hand over the steel constructed handgun safe that contained his 38 caliber Smith & Wesson revolver. His hand fit perfectly into an indented mold of a human hand that had been manufactured on top of the gun safe. He applied downward pressure to each of his fingers, one at a time, in the proper sequence that satisfied the code and activated the electronic lock. Without fail, the small metal door slammed down and revealed the handgun. Kyle reached for the already loaded weapon. Careful to keep his finger outside the trigger guard, he raced over to the bedroom door. The entire episode of him retrieving the 38 took less than twenty seconds.

The violent pounding on the bedroom door continued. "Kyle, open up! Someone's trying to break into the apartment," Angel screamed.

He opened the door and she ran directly into his arms. Angel was shaking terribly.

The faint glow from a candle, in the living room, provided enough light so that he could see down the apartment hallway.

"Angel, get under the bed and don't come out until I tell you it's safe," he ordered.

She ran to the king size bed and quickly crawled under its huge frame. She could feel her body shaking uncontrollably but could do little to stop the violent twitching.

Kyle moved rapidly down the hallway that led into the apartment living room. When he looked to his right, he could clearly see the silhouette of a person behind the vertical blinds that covered the back porch door. There had been a full moon and the light that it provided made the intruder's whereabouts quite evident. The porch door handle was jiggling, as if someone was attempting to pick the lock.

A rush of adrenalin coursed through Kyle's veins. He raised the 38 and pointed it right in the direction of the shadowy figure. "I've got a 38 pointed right at your damn head. You've got exactly five seconds to get the hell out of here before I start emptying hollow points into your skull." Kyle had yelled the words as loud as he possibly could.

Immediately, the intruder stopped working the lock. He hesitated for a second before disappearing from view. Kyle continued to stare at the porch, waiting for something unexpected to happen. After a few seconds, he slowly approached the porch door. With the 38 pointed directly at the location where he suspected the intruder might still be lurking, he focused his full attention on the door. It was so quiet that Kyle could hear the beat of his own heart as it pounded beneath his breastbone. He neither saw nor heard any additional evidence that the intruder was still present.

When Kyle finally made it to the door, he carefully pushed a few vertical blinds aside so that he could see the outside porch area. No one appeared to be there. He could see the full moon, radiating its brilliance, in the early morning sky. Kyle reached down with his free hand and tested the door handle. The lock was still secure. After he'd thoroughly convinced himself that the intruder was gone, and no longer an immediate threat to their wellbeing, he relaxed just a bit.

Kyle slowly backed away from the porch, making sure that he never removed his eyes from the back door. When he'd walked to a position, in the apartment, where he could see down the hallway to his bedroom, he called out to Angel. "It's safe, you can come out now."

Angel ran down the hall, still extremely upset from the entire ordeal. "Did you see him?" she asked.

Kyle nodded. "I saw the bastard. I don't think he'll be coming back again."

"What makes you so certain?"

"Four reasons, specifically," Kyle said.

"Four reasons?" she replied, somewhat puzzled by his answer.

"Yes, four reasons, Angel. He won't be coming back on account of you, me, Smith and Wesson." Kyle smiled as he held up the handgun to emphasize his point.

Chapter Sixteen

For the remainder of the night, Kyle and Angel slept together in the apartment living room. Kyle slept on the recliner with the 38 nearby, and Angel on the sofa. Kyle didn't believe the intruder would return again that same evening, but he wasn't taking any chances.

Kyle awoke at around 7 o'clock in the morning. He had dozed off and finally went to sleep around 3 o'clock. He looked over at Angel. She was still asleep on the sofa. A frightened kitten several hours earlier, she now seemed to be at peace with the world.

Kyle spotted the handgun on the floor next to the recliner. The sight of his weapon reminded him of the serious danger they'd faced during the previous night.

He gently got up from the recliner, being careful not to wake Angel. He knew she'd experienced a stressful night and needed the extra rest. He picked up the revolver from the floor and quietly made his way down the hall back to the bedroom.

Inside the nightstand dresser drawer, on top of the gun safe, was an ankle holster for the 38. He strapped the holster to his lower left leg and carefully placed the weapon into the holster. Kyle then put on a clean pair of blue jeans and a blue tank top.

A year earlier, Kyle had qualified for a concealed weapons permit and was legally able to carry the 38 in the state of South Carolina. Sometimes he'd carry the handgun on his ankle, but there were plenty of times that he'd leave the weapon in the safe, inside the nightstand. He initially wanted the revolver as a means of protection against a potential home invasion. Under the current circumstances, he'd made up his mind to carry the weapon from now on. He didn't know what they would encounter, in the days ahead, as they traveled the highways. The way his luck had been running, he figured it would be better for him to be armed and prepared than unarmed and vulnerable to another attacker.

The sun was shining brightly and once again it was going to be an unusually warm day for the 23 day of December. In the living room, Angel was up and moving around on the sofa.

"Kyle, where are you?" she called out.

"In the bedroom," he replied. He finished tying his white Reeboks and walked back down the hallway into the living room.

Angel was standing up, peering out the back porch door where the intruder had tried to force his way inside the apartment. She was snacking on a bag of trail mix.

"Do you see anything?" Kyle asked.

Angel turned to look at him. "No. I don't see anyone out there right now."

He walked over and gently rubbed her shoulders. "That was pretty intense last night, wasn't it?"

"I've never been so scared in my entire life," she replied.

"Angel, I think he's probably long gone."

"I didn't know that you owned a gun," she said changing the subject.

"Yeah, I purchased it at a local gun show. For the longest time, I kept it in the drawer, unloaded. Awhile back, a tenant was robbed at gunpoint; a few buildings from here, and that got me thinking that I should probably put some rounds in the thing and take it out of the drawer. I took a course last year so that I could learn how to fire it without shooting my foot off."

Angel smiled. "Is it legal for you to carry a gun in public?"

"Absolutely!" he assured her. "I qualified for a carrier's permit last year. I can legally wear the gun as long as it's concealed. I can't take it inside a bank or a government office, but I don't think any of those places will be open today."

Angel moved away from the porch door. She walked over to the dining room table and grabbed another package of trail mix before turning to confront Kyle. "Are you going to carry the gun with you today?"

"Yes, I'm going to carry the gun today. Do you have a problem with that?"

She frowned at him. "It's just that I really hate guns."

Kyle smiled. "You won't hate this gun if we're being threatened by another crazy person. You know, yesterday wasn't a particularly good day. I was shot at by a lunatic in a Li'l Cricket store and this incident, last night, could've been very serious if that guy would've picked the lock on the porch door. The way our luck's been running, it would be wise for me to carry the 38. It might end up saving our lives."

"I suppose you're right." She walked over to give him a hug. "Just promise me that you'll be careful with that thing, okay?"

He kissed Angel on the forehead and gently massaged her shoulders. "You worry too much. I want you to trust me with handling the gun. I promise to be careful and that the both of us will be perfectly safe."

Chapter Seventeen

A short distance from Kyle's apartment, the intruder was carefully hiding behind some evergreens. He looked through a pair of field glasses as Kyle and Angel walked out the front door. He watched intently as they made their way up to the parking area and got into the Chevy. From his current vantage point, he could easily follow their progress as they drove the vehicle to a parking space in front of Annie Hendrick's apartment. The intruder watched as Annie exited her apartment and climbed into the Chevy.

After they drove away, he folded the collapsible field glasses and placed them in a small leather case that was attached to a red mountain bike. He hopped on the bicycle and started to pedal down a grassy hill. He was careful to balance his body weight, on the two wheeler, as he moved over the bumpy ground. Finally, the bike's wheels made contact with the flat surface of the apartment parking lot. The intruder was able to ride the bicycle, much easier, on the smooth surface of the parking lot. Once he'd reached the parking area he quickly made his way over to Kyle's apartment building.

The intruder parked the bike on the small patio area that was directly attached to Kyle's back porch. After making sure no one was around, he began to work on the door lock that he'd attempted to pick earlier that same morning. This time he defeated the security device in just a few seconds.

The intruder entered Kyle's apartment. He quickly looked over the living room area before proceeding directly to the dining room. His eyes were immediately drawn to the copy of *Time Magazine* that Kyle had placed on the dining room table. He walked over and picked up the magazine and gently dropped the publication back on the table so that the spine of the magazine struck the table's surface first. The pages spilled open and the paper crease that had been created from Kyle and Angel constantly looking at the same few pages within the publication, caused the magazine to open up to the article titled, *December 21, 2012?* He looked at the article for a few seconds before flipping the magazine closed.

Next, he made his way down the hallway and into Kyle's bedroom. He looked at the sleigh bed and at the walnut colored dressers. He carefully opened each dresser drawer and examined its contents. He rifled through Kyle's personal belongings before replacing the pieces of property back in the same locations he'd found them. Finally, he opened the nightstand dresser drawer next to the bed. He looked inside the drawer and saw the opened gun safe. He noticed that there was no weapon inside the safe.

The intruder unclipped a two way radio from his waist belt and spoke into the device. "He's armed and I think the two of them are suspicious."

"What do you think they know?" a voice blurted out from the radio.

I don't think they know too much, but we'll definitely have to keep an eye on them. By the way, they do have a working vehicle and that's going to make them more difficult to manage."

"I'll put the word out," said the voice over the radio.

"What do you want me to do now?" the intruder asked.

"Get out of there!"

"I copy that," he said and clipped the radio back onto his belt.

Chapter Eighteen

Angel drove the yellow Chevy through the USC Upstate campus. She turned the car into the faculty parking lot and immediately spotted Paul's blue pickup truck. She decided to park her car alongside the physics professor's vehicle.

The three of them exited the Chevy and began walking to the Hodge Center. According to Kyle's watch, it was 8:45 a.m. The next press conference was scheduled to take place at 9 o'clock. Kyle and Angel had made plans, the previous day, to meet up with Paul at the press conference.

Unlike the day before, the campus seemed pretty empty to Kyle and Angel. They saw a few people moving about the university grounds but, for the most part, the place looked like a ghost town.

When they reached the Hodge Center, they found the front door locked. A red piece of paper had been taped to the front door from the inside. It was a notice explaining that the 9 o'clock press conference had been cancelled due to the fact that there were no new

93

developments to report. The notice also listed the time for the next scheduled press conference – 12 o'clock noon.

"Now what do we do?" Annie asked as she looked around the campus in different directions. She was dressed in another sweat suit. This one, lime colored, fit her much better than the mauve one she'd worn yesterday. Her makeup had been applied much neater today, and her hair had been nicely styled.

"We were supposed to meet Paul at the Hodge Center," Kyle said.

"Let's check out the science building," Angel suggested. She had on a pair of tight fitting blue jeans and a white T-shirt that had the word GAMECOCKS printed, in big red letters, on the front of the shirt.

Kyle nodded in agreement with Angel. "He's probably waiting for us in his office."

The three of them headed over to the science building. About half way there, they heard Paul's voice calling out to them from the faculty parking lot.

"Kyle, Angel, I'm over here," the professor yelled, his arms waving in the air like he was guiding a jet airliner into its parking gate.

Kyle and Angel waved back to acknowledge they'd heard him. They started walking towards the professor. The four of them finally met in-between the faculty parking lot and the science building.

Paul was excited to see them. He was sporting a brown short sleeve dress shirt, matching bowtie, light brown dress pants, and some expensive looking dress shoes. Kyle thought he looked very professor-like.

"Good morning," the professor said. He immediately acknowledged the fact that Annie had joined them. "I see you've invited another friendly face to accompany us on our journey."

Angel stepped forward and initiated the introductions. "Paul, this is Annie Hendricks. She's our friend from the apartment complex where we live. Annie, this is Dr. Paul Grossman. Paul's the physics professor we told you about last night." Angel smiled as the two strangers shook hands.

"Lovely to meet you, Annie," Paul said.

"The pleasure is all mine," Annie replied.

"I see they've cancelled the morning press conference," Kyle said. He had his thumbs shoved into the front pockets of his jeans.

"They've cancelled every press conference that's been scheduled since 6 o'clock yesterday afternoon," Paul replied. He pointed towards the campus security building. "They're becoming quite tightlipped about everything. When all this business first began, the authorities were quite generous with releasing information to campus residents. It seems to me, the campus security officers and the sheriff's office have made a collective decision not to disclose any new developments."

"Why in the world would they do that?" Annie asked. She'd been looking over at the security guards.

"They either have nothing to report or the information coming in is not very upbeat news. They probably don't want to alarm the public," Kyle explained.

"Maybe we should go over there and demand they tell us what's happening," Angel said angrily.

"They're not going to tell you anything, Angel," Paul said as he scratched the top of his head. "We'd do much better to stick to our plan and drive out to the end of the county so we can see, for ourselves, what's actually happening."

"I agree with Paul," Kyle said. He'd grown tired of trying to access information from the campus security officers and the deputies from the sheriff's office.

The four of them agreed to proceed with the original plan. They headed back to the faculty parking lot and got into the Chevy. Angel had volunteered to do the driving. Kyle was seated alongside her in the passenger seat. Annie was seated behind Angel and Paul behind Kyle in the backseat.

As Angel started the car, the elusive deputy, David, approached them on a red mountain bike. He straddled the bicycle with both legs as he leaned over to speak with Angel on the driver side of the car. He poked his head through the space created from the partially lowered car window.

"Good morning," the deputy said. "I was curious how you were able to get your car running?"

Kyle immediately leaned over towards Angel so that he could respond to the deputy. "It's been running, fine, ever since everything happened on Friday night."

The deputy smiled and adjusted his belt buckle. "Gee, that's pretty amazing considering the fact that so many of the automobiles in the county are out of commission. I guess ya'll are just lucky or something?"

"Yeah, I guess we are pretty fortunate," Kyle replied.

"Hey David," Angel said as she rolled the car window down a bit lower. "Your name is David, right?"

The deputy nodded.

"I was wondering what you were referring to, yesterday afternoon, when you made that comment to Keith, the campus security guard, about something being discovered just outside Spartanburg County? We figured that someone was going to make a comment about your remark during the press conference yesterday? Nobody said a word about any discoveries outside the county? Why is the sheriff's office holding back information?"

The deputy smiled at Angel. "The simple truth, ma'am, is that we're not entirely certain what's

97

happened. There are some theories floating around, and some information was reported yesterday afternoon, but it was later determined to be inaccurate. That's why it was never mentioned during the press conference."

"Just for kicks, what was the content of the inaccurate information?" Angel continued to press the deputy for a more detailed explanation of what was reported.

"What difference does it make? I just told you that the information was based on false reports."

"Humor me. I'd like to know what the false reports stated." Angel was irritated by the lawman.

The deputy grinned and removed his head from the car's open window. "You folks have a pleasant day and make sure you buckle up those seatbelts and drive safely." David got back on the mountain bike and proceeded to pedal his way across the faculty parking lot.

Angel looked at Kyle. "There's something definitely strange going on with that guy. He knows a lot more than he's willing to admit."

"You think?" Kyle said sarcastically. He turned around and looked at Paul. "What do you make of that?"

The professor looked perplexed. "The only thing I can tell you for certain, my boy, is that our deputy friend, David, is a really poor liar."

Perimeter

"Can we please drive, already, so we can find out what the hell's going on around here?" Annie said.

Angel grinned as she looked at her new friend in the rear view mirror. "I'm on it, Annie," she said. Angel drove the Chevy away from the campus and headed towards the Interstate.

Chapter Nineteen

Angel drove the Chevy off the campus property and onto the entrance ramp of I-85 south. She drove a few miles before taking the I-26 east exit towards Columbia. The interstate highways were littered with abandoned vehicles in all traffic lanes. The stationary obstacles made driving conditions, for her, quite challenging. She had to constantly swerve back and forth from one side of the highway to the other, in order to avoid colliding with the cars. Angel was only able to drive the Chevy at a speed of 40 miles per hour.

Kyle noticed that the car's fuel supply was still adequate. They had only used a quarter of a tank of gas since yesterday and still had just less than three quarters of a tank of gas remaining. He wasn't worried because he knew they had the garden hose, in the trunk of the car, to use as a siphoning tool. There were cars, filled with fuel, everywhere. Gasoline was going to be the last thing they'd have to worry about.

As the Chevy headed eastbound on I-26, Kyle couldn't help but notice the obvious absence of people along the road. A day earlier, they'd observed a lot of pedestrians, inside their cars and walking along the sides of the highway, while they drove on the interstate. Granted, another day had passed, and some of those people had probably abandoned their vehicles. But the roadways today, like the campus property they'd just left, had really thinned out considerably in regards to the amount of people that were visible and roaming about.

The scant numbers of people, in the area, made Kyle feel uneasy. They had already driven ten miles and he'd only seen three individuals.

"What's the matter?" Angel asked. She could tell by his facial expression that something was bothering him.

He looked over at her. "I don't know. Something doesn't seem right."

"What do you mean?"

"I feel that something is wrong."

"Wrong?" Angel looked at him. Her black hair was blowing wildly from the wind. They had lowered the vehicle's windows in order to maintain adequate air circulation throughout the car. The Chevy did not have air-conditioning, and the outside temperature was already in the mid seventies. The blowing wind made it difficult, for them, to hear one another.

"I don't know, maybe it's my imagination. It just seems like there are less people outside today. When we were at your university, for instance, I didn't see many campus residents."

"I saw some people walking around," Angel said.

"I realize that there were some people there. But compared to yesterday, the place looked pretty empty."

"Kyle, the semester just ended a few days ago. Every campus, throughout the country, clears out during the holidays."

"Look out here at the interstate," he said pointing to the roadway. "Yesterday, when we were driving, we saw people everywhere. I don't see very many people today. Where in hell did they all go? It's not as if they could get in their cars and drive away."

Angel looked out across the road. She'd been previously concentrating on not hitting the abandoned vehicles that kept coming her way. She began to focus her attention, a little more, on trying to locate people that were visible on or near the roadway. After a few minutes without seeing anyone, she finally saw a guy and a girl walking on a bridge they were about to pass beneath.

"Kyle, I see people out here. I think, maybe, you're letting your imagination get the best of you." She rolled her eyes as if to suggest he'd been overreacting.

Kyle raised the car window on the passenger side so that he could speak to Annie and Paul in the backseat. "Excuse me for interrupting, but have either of you noticed anything different about the number of people visible today versus yesterday?"

Paul stopped his conversation with Annie in mid sentence and looked at Kyle. He had a serious expression on his face. "Are you referring to the fact that there seems to be considerably less people around?"

"Yeah, I've noticed that too," Annie chimed in. She was looking out the window for signs of pedestrians. "I was going to say something to you guys before we left this morning, but I didn't want you to think I was acting kooky. I distinctly remember that on Friday night the parking lots, at the apartment complex, were filled with angry people. And there were those fights that broke out on Saturday morning, in front of our rental office. As the day progressed, I didn't see as many people walking around. Today, everything seems kind of deserted. It's kind of spooky, don't you think?"

"Angel thinks it's my imagination."

Angel frowned. "I said that I see people out here. I agree with you, Kyle, that there are definitely less people visible today as compared to yesterday. But there are still human beings walking around. A lot of people have probably moved away from the highways in order to protect themselves from the outside elements."

They continued driving down the interstate with the car windows rolled down. The temperature and humidity, inside the vehicle, were down right oppressive with them closed.

Angel reached over and gently placed her hand on the top of Kyle's left leg. He looked over and offered her a smile. It was as if the two of them had apologized to one another without having to say a word.

Suddenly, a loud bang was heard throughout the vehicle. The Chevy jerked unevenly across the road. Angel struggled to control the car. The steering wheel was fighting her like it had a mind of its own. She clutched the wheel, with both hands, and tried to successfully steer the car away from an oncoming abandoned vehicle. With all her strength, Angel was able to steer clear of a Black Ford Explorer that was sitting on the Interstate, in front of them. At last, she managed to bring the Chevy to a safe stop.

Chapter Twenty

Kyle squatted, like a baseball catcher, and viewed the Chevy's front, left tire. He ran his right hand, very carefully, over the outer surface of the blown out material.

"The treads on your tire look pretty good," he said as he stood up and looked at Angel.

"They're practically brand new tires. I only purchased them about six months ago."

Kyle looked across the road and into the surrounding woods. Although he didn't see anything that appeared to be out of the ordinary, he was suspicious of foul play.

Paul walked up behind Kyle. "Do you smell a rat?" He'd whispered the comment so that the girls couldn't hear him. He was also staring, across the highway, into the woods. The professor had been thinking along the same lines as Kyle.

Kyle turned his body away from Angel and Annie and spoke to Paul in a softer voice. "I'm thinking a gunshot from over in that direction."

Paul smiled. "I think that maybe you're right, Kyle."

"Right about what?" Annie asked. She moved her big body in-between the two men. "What's he right about, Paul?"

The professor wheeled around to look at Annie and Angel. "I was just agreeing with Kyle that the tire probably blew out from a condition known as dry rot. The tire treads look very good, but the rubber was probably filled with dry rot and the material just gave out."

"I have a spare in the trunk," Angel said. She walked over to the driver side door and retrieved the car keys. She proceeded to make her way to the back of the vehicle and opened the Chevy's trunk. She pushed the garden hose and crowbar, which Kyle had placed in the back compartment, aside and removed a black piece of carpeting that had been covering the vehicle's only spare tire.

Kyle looked in the trunk and was immediately relieved to see the spare was a real tire, not one of those temporary doughnut types, and that it was fully pressurized. He located the car's tire jack and within a few minutes had the blown out tire removed and the new one properly mounted. Kyle placed the damaged tire in the trunk and refastened the tire jack back into its proper position. He closed the trunk and looked at his watch. He smiled at his three friends. "That only took me seven minutes. It's not going to set any NASCAR records, but it isn't too bad considering the current conditions."

Angel massaged the base of her neck with her two hands. She tried shifting her head, into different positions, to workout some of the soreness she felt in her neck. The episode of the tire blowing out had really frazzled her nerves.

Kyle, an astute observer of most things, knew that Angel needed a break from driving. He walked up to her and started rubbing her neck. "Boy, you're really tight in there. Why don't you sit in the back with Annie, for awhile, and let me do some of the driving?"

"I'm okay," she mildly protested.

"Angel, you've been doing all the driving since yesterday. Please take a rest. Honestly, I'm starting to get a little car sick. It would help me out if you'd allow me to help with some of the driving."

She smiled and finally handed Kyle the car keys. "You're right. I am tired."

Kyle pulled the car's front bench seat forward and helped the girls get situated in the backseats. Once they were safely in the vehicle, Paul and Kyle climbed into the front seats.

Kyle started the Chevy and within a few seconds they were heading eastbound, once again, on I-26. Kyle figured that the 30 mile line would take them close to the town of Clinton, South Carolina. According to the last sign they'd passed, Clinton was only about 11 miles, farther, down the road.

Kyle drove the next eight miles without further incident. Kyle and Paul had noticed that the closer they got to Clinton, the less abandoned vehicles they seemed to encounter.

Paul pointed out an upcoming interstate sign. It listed the town of Clinton as being 3 miles away. Kyle slowed the car down to 25 miles per hour. He could sense, in his gut, that something was definitely wrong. The closer they got to Clinton, the more intense the uneasy feeling in Kyle's stomach became.

As they made their way down the final stretch of interstate, they encountered absolutely no abandoned vehicles whatsoever.

"Kyle, where are all the cars?" Angel asked from the backseat.

"I'm telling you, Angel, something doesn't feel right to me," he replied. Kyle kept his eyes carefully focused on the road.

Suddenly, out of nowhere, a black police helicopter appeared in the sky. It was approaching their car, head on.

Kyle slowed the Chevy down to a speed of fifteen miles per hour before hitting the brakes hard in order to bring the vehicle to a complete stop. The black helicopter was right in front of them. Kyle could see the pilot and another man seated inside the chopper. The guy who wasn't the pilot was holding up his arms, motioning for Kyle to stop the car.

The pilot landed the helicopter right on the interstate. The aircraft was only about thirty-five feet away from the Chevy.

Kyle kept his left hand on the car's steering wheel and slowly lowered his right arm so that it rested on the car seat. He wanted to be able to react quickly if necessary. The 38 revolver was loaded and strapped to his left ankle. In a normal setting, the firearm was a last resort in a no-win situation. As he sat in the car, looking at the chopper in front of him, Kyle realized that the current situation was far from being a normal setting.

"What are we going to do?" Annie asked. There was a hint of panic in her voice.

"Everybody needs to stay calm," Kyle said. He put on the most convincing smile, possible, for the benefit of the two guys inside the chopper. "Let's just see what they want."

The pilot cut the chopper's engine and the rotors on top of the aircraft began to gradually decrease their speed. After a few moments, the big blades stopped moving and hunched down a bit towards the ground. The guy opposite the pilot opened one of the aircraft's doors and began walking towards them. The way the fellow was decked out, in solid black, reminded Kyle of a black ninja fighter. He'd hoped that he couldn't fight like one.

Chapter Twenty-one

"Where you folks headed?" said the guy dressed in the black ninja suit. He stopped walking once he made his way over to the driver side of the car.

Kyle turned the Chevy's engine off and unfastened his seatbelt. The belt automatically retracted into its normal position. He kept one eye focused on Ninja Guy and the other eye on the pilot inside the chopper. "We're headed to Columbia," he lied.

The man nodded and scanned, with his eyes, the immediate vicinity around the outside of the automobile.

Kyle was now paying full attention to Ninja Guy. "Are you an officer of the law?" he asked.

"I'm with the Spartanburg County Sheriff's Office." The man reached into his back pocket and produced an open wallet that revealed a deputy's badge.

"Why'd you stop us?" Kyle asked. His left arm was lazily dangling outside the Chevy's open window. His other arm was still resting on the car seat, ready to grab the revolver, if necessary.

111

"The road's closed ahead," the deputy said. He looked back, momentarily, at the chopper, wiped a bead of sweat from his forehead, and turned back to look at Kyle. He leaned over, slightly, and poked his head through the space that was created by the car's open window. He smiled at Paul, and at Angel and Annie, in the backseat. "I can't let you folks go past this part of the interstate, for your own safety."

"Why is the road closed, officer?" Paul asked.

"Do you want the official line of bull, or would you prefer to know the truth?"

Paul laughed nervously for a moment. "I'd prefer the truth, of course."

The deputy snorted and said, "I was afraid you were going to say that. You know, the truth is not always a pretty picture. And in this particular situation that rule certainly applies."

"Has there been an accident?" Annie asked.

"Ma'am, it's very difficult for me to describe, in words, what exists, a few miles down this road."

Angel propped herself forward from the back of the car. "Deputy, we're really tired of getting jerked around by the sheriff's office. We've been getting nothing but a lot of doubletalk, for the past two days, from deputies and campus security guards at the USC Upstate campus. Can you please be honest with us? We're all big girls and boys and can handle the truth.

I'm an assistant professor of English and Paul, here, is a full professor, with a PhD in physics. Kyle and Annie are successful business people within the community. Please just tell us what's happening."

The deputy pulled his head away from the open car window. He reached for a two way radio that had been clipped to his waist belt. "This is 2122. I'm currently 3 miles from the perimeter."

After a few seconds, a voice replied. "I copy that 2122."

The deputy spoke into the radio again. "I've successfully intercepted the four occupants and their vehicle. I'm going to redirect them back to Spartanburg."

"I copy that 2122. Please advise us of any new developments."

"I'll be sure to do that," the deputy said. He backed away from the Chevy and motioned for Kyle and the others to exit the vehicle.

"You want us to get out?" Kyle asked, a bit confused by the deputy's request.

The deputy grinned. "I assume you want to know the truth about what's happening, right?"

"Hell yes," Kyle replied.

"Well, I can't show you the truth from inside the car. If the four of you exit the vehicle, it'll be a lot easier for me to give you the grand tour." The deputy clipped the two way radio back onto his belt.

Kyle and Paul got out of the car first and were followed by Angel and Annie.

Kyle looked at the deputy. "I want to show you something," he said. He walked over to the back of the Chevy and opened the vehicle's trunk. The deputy followed closely behind him. Kyle pointed inside the trunk compartment at the blown out tire. "What do you see there?"

The deputy looked in the trunk and saw the damaged tire. After a moment, he straightened his body and faced Kyle. "I want you to know that I had, absolutely, nothing to do with that."

"You know nothing about the tire blowing out?" Kyle said. His face was red with anger.

"I didn't say that. The decision to slow down your vehicle came from the county sheriff's office. I was not involved with that order. And just so you know, I disagreed with the decision in the first place."

"They could have killed all of us," Kyle said angrily. "Angel was damn lucky to keep the car from flipping over onto the highway."

The deputy nodded and looked at the four companions for a moment. After a few seconds passed, he signaled the pilot to start the chopper's engine. "Look, I told you that I had nothing to do with the tire incident. That's the simple truth. We can stand here all day long and nothing is going to change that fact.

"As you are about to find out, we have a much bigger problem to contend with. I hope that none of you are afraid of flying."

The chopper's long blades began to turn and within a short period of time the noise from the aircraft's powerful engine made it difficult to hear anything.

The deputy huddled them into a tight circle. He spoke in a loud voice as he attempted to compete with the roar of the chopper's engine. "I've got to warn you folks ahead of time that what you're about to see is disturbing. I've never seen anything like it before, and I have no logical explanation to offer you. I'll be damned if I know what's happening around here. By the way, if anyone in the sheriff's office ever found out that I'm allowing you to view the perimeter; my job would definitely be in jeopardy. Please keep that bit of information in mind.

"After having stated all of those disclaimers, if you still want to view the perimeter, let's get inside the helicopter."

Without further hesitation, they walked over to the black chopper and boarded the aircraft.

Chapter Twenty-two

Inside the chopper, the noise from the engine was even louder than when they were standing on the side of the interstate. Everybody in the aircraft had to wear blue headsets that allowed them to be able to hear one another. The headsets had microphones built into them for speaking.

"What about my car?" Angel inquired. She thought that her voice had sounded funny as she spoke into the microphone and listened to the audio signal that was reproduced through her headset.

The deputy looked back at Angel. "Your vehicle will be fine. I have a friend watching it. When we're finished with the tour, I'll make sure you're dropped off at this same location."

The chopper began to vibrate and slowly lifted away from the ground. Angel and Annie watched the Chevy grow smaller as they climbed higher in the sky.

"We're going to fly to the very edge of the perimeter line. That's as far as we can go and still safely operate the aircraft," the deputy explained.

"What do you mean when you say perimeter line?" Paul asked.

"Imagine, Professor, that you were viewing a map of Spartanburg County. If I took a drawing compass and placed a point on that map in the heart of downtown Spartanburg, and drew a circle that was 30 miles in distance from that central point, in all directions; that would represent what I'm referring to as the perimeter line."

"So are you telling us that it's unsafe to travel farther than a distance of 30 miles from the center of Spartanburg, in all directions?" Kyle asked.

"That's what I'm telling you," the deputy replied. He pointed to the distant horizon. "Basically speaking, we have followed the perimeter line and have determined it encircles all of Spartanburg County, in a thirty mile radius."

The chopper was currently flying at an altitude that placed it clearly above the forest's thick canopy of trees. As Kyle looked around, he didn't see anything that appeared to be out of the ordinary. The helicopter moved very swiftly through the afternoon sky. The trees, below, seemed to zip by at an accelerating pace.

"What are we supposed to be watching for?" Annie asked. She had been looking outside the aircraft and had both hands up against her forehead in an effort to block the sun's glare that was coming through the cockpit windshield.

"You won't be able to miss it once we get in range," the deputy replied.

"Deputy, what's your name?" Kyle asked.

The deputy smiled as he kept his line of vision directly on the horizon in front of them. "It's Adam Honeycutt."

"Well, I'm Kyle Wilson and I wanted to personally thank you, Adam, for being the only deputy, in Spartanburg County, that was willing to be honest with us."

"You might not be so thankful once you take a look at the view right over there," Adam said as he pointed to the skyline up ahead.

Kyle and Paul saw it first. Angel and Annie made visual confirmation next.

"My sweet Jesus," Angel said as she stared in total disbelief through the cockpit window. *Adam had been absolutely correct*, she thought silently to herself. It, actually, was hard to describe what she was seeing with mere words. That in itself was an amazing thing considering the fact that Angel was an assistant professor of English.

Paul's mouth was hanging wide open. If he'd been outside the chopper he would have swallowed a thousand bugs. With his eyes fixed on the sky, a number of thoughts raced through his mind. A few of them involved quantum theories that might offer a logical explanation about what he saw.

Annie rubbed at her eyes, with both hands, to make sure they weren't creating optical illusions. It was the strangest and most disturbing scene she'd ever visualized. The only thing she could think of, at the moment, was the very sad thought that her life as she'd known it for 55 years, was probably over.

As Kyle's eyes took in the bleak looking scene that filled the sky in front of them, he couldn't help but think about the article he'd recently read in the current issue of *Time Magazine*. He'd never paid very much attention to all that stuff about the Mayan calendar and the mysterious date of December 21, 2012. Most of the information he'd read about the controversial subject had lead him to believe that there was nothing, of any substance, to the legend. He felt that the 2012 date was merely a way for Hollywood to produce science fiction blockbusters, through fear mongering, and to cash in on millions of dollars. But right now, as he witnessed the extraordinary view that was in front of him, the realization that he, and millions of others, might have unfairly dismissed this subject matter without serious scientific review, and incorrectly labeled it as science fiction, began to haunt him.

Chapter Twenty-three

The pilot slowly lowered the chopper before finally setting down the aircraft on the eastbound side of I-26. Once he killed the engine, the deafening noise, that had been continuously present inside the chopper's cockpit, began to wane.

Kyle and the others removed the blue headsets they'd been wearing. After Deputy Adam opened the aircraft's side hatch, the four companions followed the lawman outside. The pilot, as he did before, remained inside the chopper's cockpit.

Kyle walked with his three friends onto the interstate highway. They positioned themselves so that they were all facing east. In front of them, they observed the smooth surface of the asphalt highway. As they followed, with their eyes, the path of the roadway eastbound, they could see the highway's progression come to, what appeared to be, an abrupt end about fifty yards away.

The interstate seemed to disappear into a white, opaque looking wall of fog. It was the densest looking fogbank that Kyle had ever witnessed. As he looked to his left and right, he could clearly see that the wall of impenetrable haze continued indefinitely from the ground all the way up to the sky.

Angel and Annie had grabbed a hold of each other's arm. They tried to understand the totally bizarre scene that stood before them. They were speechless because no words could possibly describe the indescribable.

Paul had knelt down on the road with his left knee. With his right hand positioned on his pelvis, he continued to search, his sharp scientific mind, for a logical way to explain the phenomena.

The four of them looked as if they'd just seen a ghost. They struggled to process the visual information their eyes reported. None of the images, they observed, made any sense to them whatsoever. The whiteout conditions, that currently existed, were not only intimidating in appearance, but also confusing to the primary visual centers within their brains. The normal parameters that existed within a three dimensional world ceased to exist a mere fifty yards in front of them. A human brain required, and was quite dependent on, a reality construct that was three dimensional in nature. The wall of whiteness, which stood before them, did not provide the natural visual stimuli neurophysiology demanded.

All of a sudden, Kyle had a strong urge to investigate the phenomena. He started walking slowly in the direction of the fogbank. With each step that he took, Kyle noticed a decrease in his ability to properly calculate depth perception. After he traveled about twenty yards, he couldn't be certain about how close or far away from the fogbank he actually was. Kyle continued the journey, and as he did so his sensibilities began to fade even more. He no longer was cognizant of Angel, Paul, Annie or the deputy and his pilot. It almost seemed as if he'd been invited into a brand new reality and that the five senses that he normally relied upon, to navigate successfully through the current world, were being switched off in preparation for his acclimation to a new venue.

Angel was horrified. She stood there, looking helpless, in the middle of the road, watching Kyle's figure slowly dissolve into the great wall of whiteness that was in front of them. "Isn't somebody going to stop him?" she yelled out. She turned to Paul and to Annie. "Is it safe for him to walk into that stuff?"

Hearing the alarm in her voice, Adam started jogging after Kyle. He quickened his pace from a jog to a full out sprint once he'd realized that Kyle was almost at the white wall's outermost edge.

"Stop walking into it, Kyle!" the deputy yelled out to him. He could still faintly make out the outline of his body against the white background of the fogbank. But with each step closer that Kyle moved towards the wall, his body seemed to become a little less recognizable against the enormous white background.

The deputy was trim, muscular and in good physical shape. A former track athlete at nearby Clemson University, he closed the distance between Kyle and himself in a matter of seconds.

Angel, Annie, and Paul were yelling, as loud as they could, for Kyle to turn around. The danger that had suddenly been presented to their friend seemed to wake them from a hypnotic trance the wall of whiteness had created.

"I can't see either one of them," Angel screamed. She'd lost complete sight of Kyle and Adam against the backdrop of the fogbank. She became frantic. Annie tried to comfort her. Angel's breathing and pulse rate had increased substantially. She couldn't seem to force enough air into her lungs. The combination of fear and not knowing what was taking place with Kyle and Adam made her feel weak. She felt her legs become rubbery, like they were going to give out at any moment. She fought, with every ounce of strength that she could muster, to stay upright and conscious. The next thing she knew, she had entered the fogbank. She became lost in the great wall of whiteness, looking for Kyle and Adam. She couldn't find them. It was an awful feeling to be blind and helpless. But that's what had happened to her. Angel was blind, but not in the usual way. It wasn't darkness that prevented her from finding Kyle and Adam. It was the bright whiteness that was surrounding her.

It was no use. Angel's system had begun to shut down from all the excitement. It was a combination of dehydration and emotional overload that sent her slumping towards the ground. Annie reacted quickly and caught Angel, just in time, to break her fall. Paul immediately rushed over to help. Between the two of them, they successfully placed her in a supine position on the highway.

Angel was out cold and Kyle and Adam were lost in the clouds. Annie and Paul looked up at each other as they tended to their young friend, sprawled out on the ground. Their facial expressions openly demonstrated, to each other, the horror they were experiencing. The two of them realized that they were attempting to revive a girl named Angel, but what they really needed was a small miracle!

Chapter Twenty-four

Annie and Paul had been completely preoccupied with trying to help Angel. After a few minutes, they sensed that the young English professor was beginning to breathe much easier.

Annie turned her attention, for a moment, to the fogbank. At first glance, she thought her eyes might've been playing tricks on her. "Paul," she said tapping the professor on the top of his left shoulder.

Paul looked up at her. "What is it?" he asked.

"Look over there." She pointed to the vast wall of whiteness.

As Paul turned to look at what had caught Annie's attention, he immediately saw, against the white foggy background, the contrasting silhouettes of two men walking in their direction. "Well thank God for small miracles," he said softly.

Adam and Kyle had finally found their way out of the fogbank. When Kyle saw Angel on the ground, with Annie and Paul leaning over her, he immediately started running over to his friends.

"What happened to her? Is she okay?" he asked.

"She passed out," Annie replied. She gently massaged the top of Angel's head. "I think she's going to be fine."

"I think she's starting to come out of it," Paul said trying to reassure Kyle. He picked himself up from the ground and brushed off a few pieces of loose asphalt from his knees. "We thought we'd lost you for good, my boy."

Kyle bent down to feel Angel's face. As he touched her left cheek with his hand, her eyes began to flutter. A few seconds later, she began to regain consciousness.

Angel's entire body jumped suddenly, and her eyes sprang open. "Where's Kyle?" she yelled out loud.

"Easy does it, I'm right here," he said in a soft voice. He gently stroked the top of her forehead and felt a few beads of perspiration that had formed on the surface of her skin.

"Thank God you're safe!" she cried. A few tears streamed down the sides of her cheeks. Angel was finally able to bring her eyes back into focus. The sight of Kyle made her feel stronger almost immediately.

"Are you okay?" Annie asked. She was still crouched down beside Angel. "You gave us a pretty good scare."

"I'm fine," she replied. Angel sat up from the roadway and looked over at Annie and Paul. "Thanks, you two, for looking after me."

"No problem," Annie said. She turned to look at Paul. "We knew that you'd do the same for us."

Adam had made his way over to where Angel had been sitting on the road. "Here, drink this," he said as he reached over and offered her bottled water. He'd retrieved a half dozen of them from inside the chopper.

Angel grabbed the bottled water. She started drinking the liquid refreshment profusely. She downed the entire bottle in about 30 seconds. "I'm so thirsty," she said.

"You're dehydrated," Adam explained. He tossed her another one and handed out the remaining bottled waters to Kyle, Paul, and Annie while keeping one for himself.

"Kyle, why did you start walking into that stuff?" Angel asked in-between sips of water.

"I don't know," he replied. He drank some bottled water too. "I felt drawn to it. I guess I was just overwhelmed by curiosity."

"What was it like, inside?" Paul asked.

"It was like nothing else that I've ever encountered. It was completely white, inside. I couldn't see where I was going. I became disoriented and couldn't tell what direction I needed to go in order to get out of there. I couldn't rely on my sense of direction. It's a good thing Adam grabbed a hold of me. If he hadn't spotted me, I don't know how I would've made it out of there."

"A few more steps and we might've both been lost in that soup, forever," Adam said. He smiled at Kyle. "You know, we've lost 12 deputies in two days to that giant cloud. They all tried to see what's inside, wandered in too far, and never came back out. For some reason, radios don't work inside there. Some sort of radio interference takes place once you get in past a certain point."

Paul scratched his head. He'd found the last comment that Adam made quite interesting. "Adam, are you absolutely positive that radios won't work inside that soup?"

Adam eyed the professor intently. "When the deputies went in, they each had functioning two way radios. We heard them loud and clear, at first. The farther they progressed into the fogbank, the more static became apparent. In the end, we lost radio communications with all of them. We were never successful in reestablishing contact with any of our deputies."

"What are you thinking, Paul?" Kyle asked.

The professor turned towards Kyle. "I know there's a logical explanation for all of this. There has to be. If we're going to find out what's really going on, I believe the answers will come from applying some very basic principles within the discipline of quantum theory."

"I'm sorry, professor, but you just lost me," Adam said.

Paul smiled at the deputy. "You see, Adam, in order for a properly functioning radio not to operate, there has to be some form of frequency disturbance within the white soupy stuff. The entire planet is based on frequencies. A disruption in frequencies can cause everything to go haywire."

"That's the logical explanation?" Adam said frowning at Paul. "You're saying that because a few frequencies have been disrupted, we now have New England clam chowder surrounding Spartanburg County?"

Paul's facial expression grew a bit more serious. "In a nutshell, that's what I'm saying. Let me explain it to you from the perspective of a quantum physicist."

"No disrespect to you, Professor, but I'm not too good with understanding math and physics formulas," Adam said.

"You don't have to be a mathematician to understand the theories associated with quantum physics. Everything in the universe is made up of subatomic particles. They're always moving about in all directions and at incredible rates of speed. The solid objects that make up our world are all made from millions and millions of tiny subatomic particles.

"Quantum physicists have discovered that 99 percent of the tiny particles, which are moving about at tremendous speeds, are really hollow."

"Paul, how can the subatomic particles be hollow if they're responsible for making up the larger, more solid, objects that exist in the world?" Kyle asked. Just when he thought he'd begun to understand Paul, he became confused again.

"Great question, Kyle," Paul replied. "Perhaps you should've majored in physics. The way the physicists have explained the theory is by stating that the subatomic particles fluctuate, back and forth, between being a solid particle and a wave length. At any given time, the solidness of a particle can change to a non solidified wave form and vice versa. Some of the fringe biologists, in major universities, have theorized that the DNA of human beings, and other life forms on the planet, has a dual purpose. Their theory is that the DNA not only acts as a blue print for building the physical beings that walk the planet, but that it also serves as an antenna. If you look at the structure of DNA, it can be likened to a radio receiver. It has that big double helix swirl to it, like an antenna, and some biologists believe it's really a gigantic radio tuner. The theory that has been hypothesized states that the DNA has been designed to receive certain frequencies. When it receives those frequencies, in the proper range, it turns the wave forms into the more solidified particles, and that in turn allows the hollow particles to form the very solid objects that make up our world."

"Paul, you're a really nice man," Annie said. She patted him on the back. "But I don't understand a word of what you just said."

Paul laughed. "Annie, when you're listening to your favorite station on the radio, you must realize that the other stations are also playing at the same time. Just because you can't hear them doesn't mean that they're not simultaneously broadcasting their stations' signals. Your radio allows you to tune into various radio frequencies. When you slide the radio tuner in different directions, it allows you to access different stations. Depending on which way you move the tuner, a different signal is picked up and another station can be accessed. The radio analogy I am describing is kind of similar to what the biologists believe happens when the subatomic particles interact with human DNA."

"So let me get this straight, Paul," Angel said. She stood up and stretched her arms into the air. "You're saying that what a human being sees is really a wide range of frequency fields, or wave lengths? The energy patterns are picked up and read by the DNA and transformed into the virtual reality world that you and I perceive as being solid?"

"Angel, I think you would do well in a physics curriculum as well," Paul joked.

"I think I understand, Paul," Kyle said. He was looking back in the direction of the fogbank. "You believe that whatever happened on Friday evening must've disrupted the subatomic frequencies or particles and that's why we are seeing an enormous white mass that is surrounding the entire county? Our DNA is not able to read the frequencies properly and so the world as we knew it, outside the 30 mile zone, is no longer a part of our reality?"

Paul smiled at Kyle. "You know," he said, "if you and Angel ever decide to get married and have kids, I'd put up a small wager that the children would be brilliant within the field of physics."

Chapter Twenty-five

The chopper raced back through the late afternoon sky in the direction of Angel's Chevy. Kyle sat in the cockpit with his arms resting on his lap. Lost in deep thought, he wondered if Paul's theory was the explanation they'd been searching for. It kind of made sense to him, but it still seemed very farfetched. And what if Paul's theory was correct? What would they do? Could the professor figure out a solution to the current problem that would reverse the effects of what had already happened?

Kyle looked at his three friends, seated in the cockpit, alongside him. Angel was closest to him. She looked up momentarily and they exchanged smiles. Paul and Annie were staring out the cockpit window at the tree line below.

Kyle noticed that Adam was speaking to the pilot. The two men had their backs to him and his friends. They must've had their microphones set on a different channel, because zero audio was coming through Kyle's headset.

Kyle had been confused about a few things and was curious if Adam knew additional details about those particular items. He wondered if the deputy would share that kind of information. He figured the only way he'd ever find out for sure was if he asked Adam, straight out, some very pointed questions once they landed. He'd wait until they were outside the helicopter and away from the pilot. He didn't want to ask him about sensitive information in front of his colleague.

After they landed and exited the chopper, Kyle approached Adam. "Listen," he began. "I wanted to thank you, once again, for showing us what we're up against."

"You're welcome," the deputy replied. They slowly walked away from the helicopter and the others. "I wanted to remind you that I took a big risk taking you and your friends out to the perimeter line. I could really get into a lot of trouble if certain people found out what we did today."

"What about the pilot?" Kyle asked.

"I'm not worried about Henry," Adam replied. He glanced back in the direction of his pilot. The man was busy checking over some instruments on the aircraft's control panel. "We go back a long time and he'd never say a word to anyone."

Kyle nodded. "Tell me, Adam, why is it the chopper was able to work? Why didn't it get fried like all the other machines with electronic components?"

"We had it in the vault along with three other aircrafts."

"The vault? What's that?" Kyle asked.

"It's a concrete reinforced hangar we use to protect expensive equipment during an outbreak of tornados and gusty storms. We had a few aircrafts, radios, and televisions stored in there on Friday evening. Everything inside the vault was spared from the effects of the incident."

Kyle looked over at his friends. They were congregating near the Chevy, waiting for him to return. "Adam, I wanted to ask you about something that's been bothering me since earlier today."

"What's that?" the deputy asked.

"I've noticed that there seems to be a lot less people, since yesterday, near the roadways, the university, and our apartment complex. Are you aware of any information that might possibly support my observation?"

Adam hesitated a moment before he replied. "The sheriff's office is aware of what you're speaking about."

"What's happening to these people?"

"They're disappearing! We really don't know what the hell's happening, for sure. We believe it's all tied into the fogbank and the incident that started all of this on Friday night."

"Have you actually seen anyone disappear?" Kyle asked.

"Yes. There was a lady with four children on highway 221 that disappeared. I was on a mountain bike when I spotted her. Her kids were running along the sides of the highway. I stopped to see if they were okay. When I started talking to the woman, she told me that her husband had disappeared right in front of her eyes. She said that a lot of other people, on the highway, had also disappeared. I thought she was crazy. She started talking about the Rapture."

"The Rapture?" Kyle said.

"Yeah, you know, the Rapture. A lot of Christians believe that the End Times are coming soon. The good people will be taken to heaven to live with Jesus and the Father for all of eternity."

"What happens to the bad people?"

"They get left behind and have to experience the end of the world. The people that believe in the Rapture say that the good people will suddenly vanish. It's supposed to happen really fast. According to many religious leaders, the people left behind will only find the clothes and personal belongings of those chosen to live in heaven."

"Do you believe that's what's happening?"

Adam smiled at Kyle. "I don't have any other explanation at this stage of the game.

"Anyway, I was talking to this woman on Highway 221, and her kids were running all over the road. She explained to me that their car broke down on Friday evening and they became stranded. The husband went for help. She explained that as he began walking down the road, away from them, he faded out of view."

Kyle laughed nervously. "He faded out of view, like on Star Trek when they used to beam the crew to a distant planet?"

"Yes," Adam replied.

"I turned around to get a notepad and a pen, from my bike, to take down the woman's information. When I turned back around to speak to her, she and the kids were gone. They'd vanished into thin air—like the Rapture!"

"But did you, actually, see them disappear?" Kyle asked.

"No. I didn't see them disappear. But I only had my back turned for a few seconds. I want you to understand that I'm not exaggerating one bit. Those people were there, in front of me, one second and gone the next."

Kyle shook his head in disbelief. "Why is the sheriff's office so damned determined to prevent people from finding out the truth about what's happened? I don't understand the secrecy thing?"

"I think the sheriff and other county officials are afraid of wide scale panic. We still don't understand what we're dealing with. We're in uncharted waters. Besides, we're dealing with a more serious problem at the moment."

Kyle looked at the deputy curiously. "What are you talking about?"

Adam looked, briefly, in the direction of the others, standing near the Chevy. "The more pressing problem is that fogbank we visited today. It's slowly advancing in the direction of downtown Spartanburg."

"How slowly is it advancing?" Kyle asked.

"About 800 feet a day," the deputy replied.

Kyle scratched his head. "That's a little over a mile each week. That's not very slow, Adam. We only have 30 miles to play with. Is it advancing, towards the city, from all directions?"

"That's what we think."

Kyle was visibly upset. "We've got to do something! The sheriff's office has to inform everybody about what's going on. Maybe, if they'd include more people in their circle of knowledge, there'd be a better chance of someone coming up with a solution to this nightmare?"

"Listen Kyle, you'd better cool it. The sheriff's office is keeping you under surveillance. They know that you and your girlfriend have a working automobile. From what I've heard, they're watching your apartment."

"Dammit! Did you know someone tried to break into my apartment last night? I thought the police were supposed to arrest the home invaders, not impersonate them?"

"I haven't heard anything specific in regards to breaking into your apartment, but it wouldn't surprise me to find out they'd done something stupid like that. They're really spooked, right now. They know you're snooping around, asking questions, and more important, they know that you have a set of wheels and can get around. For your own safety, be careful."

Adam and Kyle walked back to where the Chevy was parked.

"It's nice of you boys to join the common people," Annie said.

Kyle smiled at her. "I was speaking with Adam about a few things. I'll fill everyone in, about what we discussed, on the ride back to town."

Paul stepped forward to address the deputy. "Adam, is there any television equipment, you're aware of, that's still in good working order?"

Adam looked at the professor curiously. "I might be able to get my hands on a television set."

"If you can, I'd like to conduct an experiment back at the fogbank, tomorrow."

"What kind of experiment?" Kyle asked.

"The kind of experiment that might save our lives."

"I don't understand, Professor," Adam said.

"It will be the most important experiment I've ever performed. We'll also need some additional equipment."

"What kind of additional equipment?" Angel asked.

"We're going to have to find a small generator, a remote controlled satellite dish, some electrical cords and TV cables."

"That's a pretty tall order, Professor," Adam said.

"I understand that. But I can assure you that the end result will pay us huge dividends. I already have an important piece of technology that will help us to accomplish the experiment's goals."

"What kind of technology might that be?" Annie asked.

"I have a homemade amplifier board that we are going to utilize if my little experiment turns out to be successful. You see, I think it's quite possible to capture television signals that are inside the fogbank."

"You think there are active television transmissions taking place in the fogbank, Paul?" Kyle inquired.

"I believe the fogbank is preventing us from receiving television, as well as other, signals from the outside world. But if we can, somehow, get a satellite dish into that soup, and link a television to it, we might be able to tune into some frequencies from the other side."

"The other side of what?" Angel asked.

"The other side of an alternate reality that's inside that fogbank," Paul replied.

Chapter Twenty-six

On the ride back from the perimeter line, Kyle provided his friends with an extensive summary of what he and Adam had discussed after they exited the chopper. He went into great detail about the woman who'd disappeared on Highway 221. He also told them that the sheriff's office was aware of the fact that people were disappearing from different areas within the county. The one thing that concerned all of them was the discovery the sheriff's office had made about the fogbank moving towards the city of Spartanburg.

Before they headed back to Kyle's apartment, Angel pulled the Chevy into the parking lot of a nearby Super Walmart store that had been giving away food rations. Deputy Adam had told them about the food distribution program earlier in the day. Fortunately, they'd made it to the store location before the last of the rations had been handed out. Deputies, from the sheriff's office, had been assigned to help distribute food at different store locations.

The lines to obtain the ration packages were not very long. Kyle had been surprised to find such a low turnout of people at the store. Anyone willing to put up with the short lines was rewarded with valuable groceries.

When they finally reached the front of the line, each of them received a small plastic shopping bag filled with a can of chicken soup, a can of corn, a box of cereal, a few pouches of tuna fish, Saltine crackers, peanut butter, and two bottled waters. The deputies had informed them that the program would continue every afternoon between the hours of 3 o'clock and 6 o'clock, for as long as supplies lasted.

After they arrived at the apartment, Kyle, Angel, Annie, and Paul prepared the food they'd received at the store on the outside grill. After dinner, they sat around Kyle's dining room table discussing the events that had transpired earlier in the day.

"In my opinion, it just doesn't make any sense to keep the community in the dark about everything that's been discovered," Kyle said.

"I agree," added Angel. She was using a butter knife to spread some peanut butter across the sides of two Saltine crackers and preparing to make a sandwich out of the two halves. "The sheriff's office is not handling this properly."

"I'm scared that I might dissolve into thin air at any moment," Annie said. "I know what you guys are thinking." Annie laughed as she pointed to her slightly overweight body. "I know that I'm a little thick in some places, but I'm still scared! Where the heck are all these people disappearing to?"

"I think what's happened here is absolutely fascinating," Paul explained. The gears in his mind were turning again. "I'm convinced that whatever occurred on Friday evening must have interrupted the normal particle frequencies that make up our physical surroundings. For some strange reason, everything outside of our 30 mile area has apparently gone haywire."

"Paul, why do you think the frequencies are still working properly inside Spartanburg County?" Angel asked.

"There are a couple of possibilities. The first one being that the frequencies within our area might have been spared from some major traumatic event that has affected every other location in the state of South Carolina, and maybe even the entire planet. We really don't know, for sure, because we don't have access to media coverage that could give us important insight on how other locations are doing.

"Another possibility might be that the frequencies outside the perimeter line are functioning in a normal capacity, and that our area has been affected by a very traumatic event that is currently interfering with our abilities to properly tune into the outside frequencies. This, in my opinion, makes more sense because of the simple fact that we witnessed the brilliant flash of light on Friday night which seemed to trigger this whole fiasco."

"Paul, do you think those are the only two scenarios that might be taking place here?" Kyle asked. He looked attentively at the professor.

"There is one other possibility," Paul said as he sipped on some bottled water. "Whatever occurred on Friday night might have destroyed or slightly tweaked the DNA in our bodies. If that's the case, we may no longer be able to perceive the particle frequency transmissions that normally surround us. Our collective abilities to perceive, what we are used to calling, everyday reality might have been permanently damaged. A cataclysmic event might have brought with it a lot of electrically charged energy. That energy might have temporarily frozen a small defined area of subatomic particles, inside our 30 mile area. In time, those particles will, most likely, melt from the electric frost that's affected them. Once the melt begins, we'll probably lose our current abilities to perceive frequencies within the county."

"What would happen to us if that, actually, was the case?" Annie asked. She stopped spreading peanut butter across a cracker for a moment.

Paul looked at her with a somber expression plastered across his face. "It wouldn't be a good prognosis. In fact, the melt might already be occurring. This might be why the fogbank is slowly advancing towards the city of Spartanburg."

Angel stood up and began pacing back and forth in the apartment living room. "Paul," she said, "there's got to be some way to undo the damage that's been done. I can't believe, in that brilliant head of yours, there's not a solution to our situation."

Paul laughed nervously. "I don't want to get everybody's hopes up, Angel. There's a theoretical construct that could possibly reverse the entire process. From a quantum theory perspective, it could definitely work. So, yes, there is something I've been kicking around. That's why I asked for the television set, the satellite dish, and the generator."

"Adam told me he'd definitely have the equipment you requested by tomorrow morning," Kyle said.

"That's good! By the way, we'll need to stop at the university, in the morning, before we leave for the perimeter line again. I need to pick up my amplifier board."

"I know you explained it to me before, Paul, but can you tell me why you need the amplifier?" Annie asked. She was spreading peanut butter on the Saltine crackers again.

"I want to use the amplifier to, hopefully, reverse what's happened to us. Once I'm able to establish a connection with some healthy frequencies, inside the fogbank, I'll attempt to draw them into our 30 mile area with a satellite dish. When I invite the healthy frequencies in, I'll use the amplifier board to boost their intensity throughout the entire 30 mile area. The amplified frequencies should, in theory, interact with the damaged or frozen subatomic particles that are currently inside the county. I believe the amplified frequencies will mend the damaged particles. The frequencies from inside the fogbank should fill into our area, creating healthy frequencies throughout Spartanburg County."

"Then everything will be fixed, right?" Annie said as she swallowed another cracker.

"Not exactly," Paul replied. He shifted his body weight in the chair and took another sip of bottled water. "My theory is predicated on another biological concept that is considered fringe science by many. The concept theorizes that the particle frequencies surrounding us also directly influence the DNA in our bodies. In other words, as the frequencies are modified in our immediate environment, they will greatly

147

influence change within the structure of our DNA. If the theory is correct, and I believe that it is, the amplified frequencies, which we draw into the Spartanburg area, will automatically repair any human and animal DNA that might have been damaged from Friday night's event."

"This all sounds a little out there, Paul. Do you think it will actually work?" Angel asked.

The professor downed the remainder of his bottled water and placed the empty container on the dining room table. He looked at Angel and the rest of his friends before he spoke. "Honey, for all of our sakes, it had better work."

Chapter Twenty-seven

Angel, Annie, and Paul had camped out at Kyle's apartment the previous night so that everybody could get an early start the following morning. It was December 24, the day before Christmas. They'd made plans to meet up with Adam at an elementary school located behind the apartment complex at 10 o'clock in the morning. Adam planned to have his pilot friend, Henry, land the police helicopter on a football field, adjacent to the school building.

After eating a breakfast that consisted of some dry cereal, trail mix, and Saltines covered with peanut butter, the professor and Kyle drove the Chevy to the USC Upstate campus to pick up the electronic amplifier Paul had designed.

Annie and Angel decided to stay behind at Kyle's apartment so that they could pack some bottled water into a red cooler that Angel retrieved from her apartment.

During breakfast, Paul had advised his friends to begin drinking a lot of water. He'd convinced himself that dehydration was the primary culprit that triggered the disappearance of so many people. His theory was based on their collective understanding that most of the people missing were last observed on the roadways. A lot of these individuals had one thing in common. They had been subjected to prolonged periods of sun exposure, without having anything to drink. The people that had been stranded, since Friday night, were forced to endure the warm Carolina weather while staying on or near the hot asphalt surface of the highway. Paul realized that, under normal circumstances, a state of mild dehydration would not present the human body with a significant challenge. But these weren't normal circumstances. Because the subatomic particles surrounding them were quite unstable, and because so many people in the community had compromised DNA, the mild states of dehydration people experienced placed enough stresses on their physiology to begin affecting DNA molecules. The unique combination of altered states of biology and environment were causing people to dissolve into thin air.

When Kyle and Paul drove onto the university property, they found very few people walking around. Even the main security building looked abandoned, and there were no campus security officers stationed outside.

The front entrance to the Horace C. Smith Science Building was locked. Fortunately, Paul had a key that unlocked the door. Inside, the facility was dark and the smell of chemicals still permeated the air. When they reached Paul's office, the professor flipped on a switch that was inconspicuously positioned under the corner of his desk. A small battery operated light bulb dimly lit the room.

Paul moved some books and a few folders away from the wall that was directly opposite the front of his desk. He reached down and picked up a tiny suit case and placed it on top of the desk. He opened the lid and gently pulled out a circuit board that was about the size of a standard piece of kitchen, ceramic tile. The green board was littered with diodes, capacitors, resistors, and transistors. The pieces were clumped together so closely that it reminded Kyle of a bird's eye view of a modern city landscape. The numerous components were bridged together by various points of solder. The entire circuit board looked, quite sophisticated, like the work of a genius.

"Paul, can I ask you a dumb question?" Kyle said as he peered down at the circuit board.

The professor gently placed the device back into the tiny case and shut the top. "There are no dumb questions," he replied.

"When you're not using your amplifier to save the city of Spartanburg from subatomic particles that have gone haywire, what function does it serve?"

"It's Tesla technology!"

"Tesla technology?" Kyle asked slightly confused.

"Nikola Tesla was a great inventor, mechanical, and electrical engineer. He was eons ahead of his time. Much of his work was stolen by our government and hidden from society. This amplifier is one of his original designs." Paul looked down at the suit case and tapped it gently with his right hand. "This instrument can take any frequency, signal, or electric current and boost its intensity a million times. If I hooked a small power source to her, I could turn on all the lights in this building. I could power up the entire campus, or even a city. This little circuit board could put all the oil companies out of business in one week's time. Of course you'd need to have functional electronic components, within the city limits, that have not been fried." He smiled at Kyle.

"You got this amplifier from Tesla, Paul?"

"No. I was given the schematic design, for the device, by a young man about 10 years ago. He'd received it from some people that had been close friends with a physicist that had a good understanding of Tesla's work. I built the circuit board from scratch, using Tesla's schematic."

"Have you ever used it before?"

"Yes! It works very well. I've had to be extremely careful, over the years, not to disclose it to anyone. If the wrong people would've discovered that I had a circuit board like this, my life would have been in grave danger."

"Why is it, Paul, that your electronic amplifier still works while everything else, which uses electric, is fried and completely useless?"

"I designed the suit case so that it was insulated with a synthetic polymer that protects sensitive electronics."

"Oh, of course, that makes perfect sense. I should have realized that everyone has a suit case like that hanging around." Kyle stared at Paul for a moment and grinned. "It almost seems as though you were anticipating Friday night's event?"

Paul waved his hand dismissively at Kyle before he fetched the suit case from the top of the desk. He chuckled slightly and said, "This is a very important piece of equipment. You can never be too careful, my boy."

Chapter Twenty-eight

When Kyle and Paul returned to the apartment, Annie and Angel had already finished packing the red cooler with bottled water. While the guys were at the university, picking up the amplifier, the girls had been busy completing their own chores. They'd made it a priority to walk over to Annie's apartment and retrieve an unopened case of Deer Park spring water from the kitchen. Annie had purchased the water on Friday afternoon, before any of the strangeness had begun.

Between Annie's stash, the half dozen bottles they'd found at Angel's place, and the remaining inventory in Kyle's kitchen, the girls felt confident about having enough bottled water to keep everybody adequately hydrated.

Angel had been spooked, earlier, by Paul's comments during breakfast. His strange theory about dehydration, being the likely reason why people were dissolving into thin air, was instrumental in getting her motivated to secure as much bottled water as possible.

Angel was going to make damn sure that she didn't let herself become dehydrated for a second straight day.

It was fast approaching the time for the four of them to begin making their way over to the elementary school that was behind the apartment complex. In less than thirty minutes, Adam and Henry would be landing the chopper on the football field.

As they walked across the apartment complex parking lot, Kyle and Angel each grabbed an end of the red cooler. It was much too heavy to be carried by one person. Annie had a hold of a paper bag filled with some food supplies, and Paul clutched the small brown suitcase that protected Tesla's amplifier. Slowly, they walked to the end of the parking lot and followed a narrow pathway that had been carved into a wooded area that butted up against the apartment complex. At the end of the pathway, they came to a large chain link fence and a gate that separated the school's property from the apartment complex. A padlock had been inserted through the gate's latch. Kyle pulled down on the *Master Lock* several times. It was useless; the lock wasn't going to open.

Kyle quickly assessed the situation. He came to the conclusion that although he and Angel could probably climb the fence without too much of a problem, Paul and Annie didn't have the physical strength to do the same. He scanned, with his eyes, the top of the fence. It was covered with barbed wire for as long as he could see. He frowned. Kyle figured that there were only two ways to successfully open the gate. The first option was to insert the appropriate key into the padlock. Unfortunately he didn't have that key. The second option was to blow a hole into the lock with his 38 caliber revolver.

Kyle turned towards his friends. "I'm going to need everybody to stand in back of me about thirty feet or so and take cover." He pointed to a large pine tree that was situated near the narrow path they'd just walked through.

"What are you going to do?" Annie asked.

Kyle reached down and lifted his left, blue jean pant leg, revealing the 38 that was strapped to his ankle. He pulled away the Velcro strap that secured the weapon in its holster and grabbed the gun carefully, pointing it towards the ground. "I'm going to open the *Master Lock*," he explained.

"Please be careful, Kyle," Angel said. Her strong concern for his immediate safety was apparent to everyone.

"Annie, do you have any napkins in that bag of supplies?" Kyle asked.

Annie looked at him strangely. She reached inside the bag and pulled out a napkin. "Here," she said holding her arm out so that Kyle could grab it. "What's the napkin for?"

He tore the napkin into two halves, crumpled the pieces, and shoved them in his ears. "This gun's extremely loud when it's fired. I want to make sure my ears are protected. You'll all need to place your fingers into your own ears to block out the sound when I fire the weapon."

Angel, Annie, and Paul retreated down the path and got behind the large pine. Once Kyle gave the signal, they protected their ears, as he'd instructed them.

Kyle stepped, a few feet, away from the gate and slowly raised the gun towards the *Master Lock*. He cocked the 38's hammer back into position which greatly reduced the amount of pressure he'd need to apply to the trigger with his finger. Kyle inhaled and exhaled, letting all the air out of his lungs, so that he could steady his arms in an effort to create the best possible chance to strike the target. His finger twitched, the hammer sprang forward and the gun exploded. A small flame was visible, for a second, on the weapon's side. The bullet nailed the *Master Lock,* dead center, instantly producing a gaping hole in its metal base.

Kyle reached out, with his hand, and tested the lock again. He pulled down on the piece of metal as he did before. This time the lock opened. He removed the pulverized lock and dropped it on the ground. After he secured the 38 back into his ankle holster, he waved to his friends letting them know it was safe to return.

When they made their way back to the gate, Angel bent down and picked up the destroyed lock from the ground. She ran her fingers over the huge hole that the bullet had produced. She shook her head in amazement. "It's really unbelievable how powerful that little gun is."

"It got the job done," Annie said. She'd walked alongside of Angel and Kyle. Annie pointed to the school building that was directly in front of them. "We'd better get moving because that chopper will be here in a few minutes," she reminded them.

Chapter Twenty-nine

When they arrived at the school football field, it was exactly 10 o'clock in the morning. Kyle and Angel placed the cooler, filled with bottled water, on the ground near the north end zone. Annie and Paul were both physically exhausted. Paul was so tired that he sat down on the field's grassy Bermuda surface. Annie was also exhausted and, moderately, out of breath from walking the distance between Kyle's apartment and the school property. The school wasn't that far away from the apartment complex, only about a half mile, but because Annie wasn't used to regularly participating in physically demanding activities, she was suffering some physical discomfort in her leg and lower back muscles.

Although the temperature was a bit cooler than the previous few days, it still didn't feel like it was Christmas Eve Day. Kyle guessed that the temperature was somewhere in the upper sixties and that the humidity was unusually high.

Angel opened up the cooler and pulled out four bottled waters. She passed them out to everybody and kept one for herself. "I think we should drink in order to keep hydrated," she said.

They each opened a bottle and guzzled down the water. After they'd finished, Angel collected the empty bottles and ran them over to a trash receptacle that was located nearby.

In the distance, Annie could make out the faint sound of an approaching helicopter. "I think I hear them coming," she announced to the others.

Kyle had also heard the helicopter. Within a couple of minutes, the chopper's engine grew much louder. Suddenly, the four of them were able to see the black aircraft as it moved across the sky, in their direction. The chopper gradually decreased its altitude and circled around the football field before landing in a patch of grass on about the 20 yard line.

Adam opened the cockpit hatch and exited the chopper. He lowered his head slightly, acknowledging the menacing blades that were cutting through the air above him, as he made his way onto the football field and approached Kyle and the others.

"Are you guys ready?" the deputy yelled as he shook Kyle's hand. The noise from the chopper made it hard to have a conversation.

"I think we're ready," Kyle shouted. He cupped both of his hands around his mouth while speaking in an effort to try and make it easier for the deputy to hear him. "Were you able to get the equipment the professor wanted?"

Adam smiled. "I found him a television, and a moveable satellite dish."

"What about the generator?" Paul asked as he joined the conversation between Kyle and Adam.

"Professor, I was able to get you a very nice gasoline powered, generator. It's got a 6 gallon tank and it'll run continuously for about nine hours. I had it dropped off earlier, along with the other equipment you requested, at the site where we'll be landing.

"If you guys don't mind, I'd appreciate it if we could get in the chopper. The dust that's being churned up out here is killing my sinuses."

The helicopter blades were kicking up a lot of dirt and loose stones at this point. Annie had to tightly grip the paper bag she'd been carrying so that the napkins and other supplies inside wouldn't blow all over the field.

Kyle ran back over to Angel to lend her a hand with the cooler. The two of them picked up the container, filled with bottled water, and carried it onto the chopper. Paul helped Annie to climb into the cockpit. Once the four of them were inside, Adam closed the hatch and the aircraft pulled away from the ground. Within a few seconds, the black chopper was streaking across the sky, high above the city of Spartanburg, on its way back to the perimeter line.

Chapter Thirty

Henry set the chopper down about 60 yards from the perimeter line. He flipped a switch, on the cockpit's control panel, which shut off the aircraft's engine. As the huge blades, above them, began to slow down, Adam and his four guests exited the aircraft through the right side hatch.

Once they cleared the area where the chopper had landed, the five of them began walking in the general direction of the fogbank. The magnificent wall of whiteness looked just as intimidating, to Kyle, as it did less than 24 hours earlier.

Adam had strategically placed the television set and some other equipment, the professor had requested, in a safe location away from the fogbank. Once Paul checked over the inventory, he and the others began hooking up the television to the satellite dish. Next, they wired the television to the generator. Adam and Kyle walked, cautiously, towards the fogbank with the wired satellite dish. The plan was to get the dish as close to the perimeter line as possible. Once they reached the cloud formation's wall, they gently set the dish onto the roadway. As they walked away from the fogbank, they inspected the cable wire, which connected the satellite dish to the television, one last time.

Paul, Angel, and Annie were crouched down beside the small circuit board that was positioned inside the open suitcase. Paul made the final connections between the television set, the gasoline powered generator, and the circuit board.

Paul stood up and looked over the entire setup. He walked back and forth, following the cables in various directions. He checked and obsessed over the specific connection points that tied the series of wires and cables together. After a few minutes, he returned to where the others were standing, alongside the generator. "We're ready to go," he reported.

Adam walked over and pulled the cord to start the generator. The first pull didn't illicit much of a response from the engine. The second pull caused the motor to sputter a bit. The third pull did the trick. The generator sprang to life. The noise from the motor mimicked the sound of a small lawnmower. Within a few seconds, electric was flowing through the cables and the entire system was live.

Paul turned on the television. The screen instantly displayed a picture filled with various patterns of electronic snow.

"Now what?" Annie asked as she looked over at Paul. "It looks like someone forgot to pay DirecTV."

A look of excitement was visible on the professor's face. He smiled as he turned to face his friends. "Now we wait for the advancing fogbank to engulf the satellite dish. Once the dish is in the soup, the adventure will have begun."

Chapter Thirty-one

At 12 o'clock noon, the fogbank completely swallowed the satellite dish. As each hour passed, the massive structure continued to creep towards the city of Spartanburg.

The five of them stood huddled around the 34 inch television screen. Paul was busy maneuvering the satellite dish up and down and from side to side. He did so by pushing and pulling on a joystick that was directly linked to a tiny motor that had been mounted to the satellite dish.

By 12:30 in the afternoon, the television was still showing a full screen of interference. Then, out of nowhere, the image of electronic snow was suddenly replaced with the crisp, clear image of the famous news anchorman, Rex Handler. They had somehow managed to tune into SNN. Rex was dressed in a dark blue suit and was wearing a red tie. He was walking back and forth in the part of the studio that the satellite news giant referred to as *The Command Center*.

Angel hugged Kyle, excited that Paul's spaghetti collection of wires and cables had actually worked. "That's Rex Handler! That's SNN!" she yelled out to the others.

Annie was excited as well. "Paul, you're a damn genius. You actually got this pile of junk to work." She reached over, grabbed the professor, and kissed him on the cheek.

Paul was too absorbed in his work, at the moment, to worry about being congratulated. He continued working the joystick that maneuvered the satellite dish. His goal was to improve the TV's reception. With his right index finger, he nudged the joystick slightly to the left and the picture's quality faded a bit. His friends moaned in disapproval. He tapped the stick again, only this time, in the opposite direction and the picture's quality improved dramatically. The fine tuning he'd performed also activated the audio portion of the telecast.

"Quiet everybody," Adam said as he pushed a button on the TV that controlled the volume. He raised the audio to the highest setting possible. The five of them had their eyes glued to the TV screen.

Rex Handler was coming through loud and clear. "...Matt had, in fact, reported a similar occurrence last evening. And if my memory serves me correctly, some earlier reports, from Friday night, had alluded to the fact that there were multiple locations affected along the eastern seaboard, within the United States.

"Let's take a look at the latest calculations that have been compiled by NASA satellite imagery. If you look at the graphic on your screen, right now, you will see a blue map representing the United States. The areas that have been marked in red, on the map, represent locations that have suffered direct impacts from the meteor storm on Friday evening. As you can see, the states of Virginia, North Carolina, the Upstate of South Carolina, Tennessee, Kentucky, Georgia, and Florida were all hit extremely hard from the first wave of debris that entered the Earth's atmosphere.

"Now, if we turn our attention to the middle of our country, we can see that North Dakota, South Dakota, Nebraska, Oklahoma, and Texas were states that received direct impacts from a second wave of debris that took place about a half hour after the initial firestorm began.

"Reports of a third wave that affected Oregon, Nevada, and southern portions of California began pouring into our studios about one hour after the initial wave of terror was inflicted on the east coast. It's safe to say, the damage has been widespread and very severe in many locations throughout the United States.

"Right now I want to show viewers a graphic that was compiled by NASA..." The anchorman paused for a moment. He placed a hand up to his right earpiece and looked into the television camera for some added dramatic effect. "Okay, were going to switch gears here for just a second. We have Matt Oliver on the phone and he's made his way up the road from our Atlanta based studios to the Upstate of South Carolina where there were reports of severe damage from the first wave of debris. Matt, can you hear me? Matt? Matt, are you there?"

"I hear you Rex, loud and clear," said the voice of Matt Oliver. The audio was coming in extremely clear over the television. The SNN logo was now visible on the lower right portion of the television screen, and a still shot of Matt was currently occupying the remainder of the screen. "I am currently reporting to you from the community of Anderson, South Carolina. I am on Interstate 85 in the northbound lane. For those of you not familiar with this stretch of highway, let me help you to get your bearings. I-85 begins in the state of Virginia and runs in a southwestern direction through the states of North Carolina, South Carolina Georgia, and Alabama. I am currently located about 120 miles northeast of Atlanta, Georgia and 130 miles southwest of Charlotte, North Carolina.

"I've had an opportunity to view some photographs taken from this very hard hit region. What I saw was difficult for me to comprehend."

Rex's voice cut into the telecast for a moment. "Matt, can you describe, for our viewers, what you have been able to observe from your current location in Anderson, South Carolina?"

"Rex, it looks as if a war has taken place throughout the entire region. As we made our way up the interstate, we saw isolated areas of damage, fire, and even some trees that had been knocked down. When we got into the city limits of Anderson, South Carolina, the level of destruction increased tenfold. There are fires burning everywhere, and people running around screaming. The local and state police have issued a 7 o'clock curfew for all citizens. Right now, there are dozens of military helicopters flying overhead and a number of National Guard units have been deployed in an attempt to establish a *no pass zone* several miles north of here, along the Interstate 85 corridor."

Rex cut into the telecast once again. "Matt, why do you think the National Guard troops are attempting to establish a *no pass zone*, slightly north of your current location?"

Matt continued reporting. "According to the South Carolina State Police, an area north of here took on a direct hit from a meteorite. They have stated, for the record, that the location has been completely destroyed. I've confirmed that same story with the Anderson

County Sheriff. He has told me that Spartanburg County has been completely destroyed by a meteorite. The sheriff said he was on board a helicopter, which flew over Spartanburg County, and that there's nothing left there, except a huge crater. Current GPS tracking stations are confirming that from the center of downtown Spartanburg, extending in a thirty mile radius, there are no signs of life whatsoever."

Rex Handler cut back into the telecast and the picture on the TV screen shifted back to the SNN studio inside *The Command Center*.

"Thank you Matt Oliver for that report. We will touch base with you again in just a few minutes.

"It's been a terrible few days for the people of this great country as well as for the rest of our planet. We have to remember that Friday night's horrific events had far-reaching effects all over the world. Reports of similar destruction have come in from Europe, China, South America, Australia, and Africa. We believe there are other areas that have also been affected.

"We're going to step away, for a few moments, in order to have a station break. Please stay tuned to your television as SNN continues to bring you up-to-the – minute news coverage of this very tragic story. I'm Rex Handler, and we're inside *The Command Center*."

Chapter Thirty-two

Confused and upset by what she'd seen on the television, Angel knelt down on one knee.

Kyle walked over to comfort her. He placed his hands on her shoulders and began massaging them.

Annie was all over Paul. She wanted answers to questions that were forming inside her head. "What does this all mean, Paul?"

The professor looked up from the joystick he'd been holding. He carefully placed the device on the ground and walked over to Annie and the others.

Adam who'd gone back to converse with Henry, in the chopper, returned with the pilot by his side. From the expression on their faces, it was apparent to everybody that the two men were upset by the news reported on the telecast. Adam obviously relayed the details, of what had transpired, to the pilot.

Paul addressed the group. "I've suspected, from the beginning, that something terrible happened on Friday evening." He placed his hands on his hips. "Our entire area has, apparently, been wiped out. All life has been destroyed when viewed from our former perspective of reality."

"What does that mean, Paul?" Kyle asked.

"It means that we're dead! It means that everybody in Spartanburg County is dead!"

Annie moved her large frame in front of the professor. "How can we be dead if we're having a conversation, Paul? I'm breathing air for Christ's sake. Dead people don't breathe air, do they?"

"Annie, have you ever met a dead person before? How do you know dead people can't carry on conversations or that they can't breathe?"

Annie was confused by Paul's strange response.

Kyle stopped massaging Angel's shoulders and walked over to where Paul was standing. "Do you honestly believe that we're dead, Paul?"

"I do, Kyle." He paused and looked over at the fogbank. "Being dead doesn't mean that we cease to exist. That's the nonsense we've been fed since we were small children. Obviously, as everyone can see, death takes on a much different appearance once you've had an opportunity to experience it, firsthand."

"Professor, what do you think will happen to us?" Adam asked.

Paul smiled. "To tell you the truth, I don't foresee it being the doom and gloom situation that you're probably thinking it is.

"When I explained my theory about subatomic particles, I was actually discussing what I believed was happening to us. Yes, we're dead, but only from the perspective of the world that we just left. We're still very much alive. We just exist in a slightly different frequency range than before. We cannot access our previous understanding of reality and the people living in that frequency range cannot tune into our perception of reality. I can assure you, however, that the frequencies from both realities are swirling around, somewhere, in that soup." Paul was pointing to the fogbank. "There are millions of frequencies in there and that means there are also millions of alternate realities waiting to be accessed."

Angel stood up from the road and looked at the professor. "Paul, do you think we can, actually, find a new home in an alternate reality?"

Paul smiled at her. "I know that we will, Angel."

"But how can you be so damn certain that everything will turn out okay?"

"Because you said so in this letter that you wrote to me." Paul reached into his shirt pocket, pulled out an old looking envelope and handed it to the English professor.

Chapter Thirty-three

Angel stared at the envelope that Paul had handed her. The professor's name was written on the front side of the document, in her own handwriting. As she looked at the paper, a strange feeling entered her body. The feeling only lasted for a few seconds. But while it was present, Angel experienced a feeling of familiarity in regards to what Paul had been discussing. But now the feeling was gone. She looked at the professor, the envelope, and finally at Kyle.

"Open the envelope and read the letter, Angel," Paul encouraged her. "When you read what you wrote, you'll understand everything more clearly."

Kyle moved over to where Angel was standing. He looked down at the envelope. "Read it, Angel," he said.

She slowly opened the parcel and pulled out a piece of lined paper that had writing on both sides. It was a letter addressed to Paul. Angel read it aloud so that everybody could hear.

Dear Paul,

Although you don't know me, I feel that I know you very well. I am writing this letter because you asked me to do so in another place and time. I hope that what I am about to put down on paper will somehow make sense to you.

When we met, for the very first time, you explained a theory, to me, about particle-frequency fluctuation. You stated that there were millions of frequencies present in our surrounding environment and that the human DNA was able to read those frequencies and turn them into our very own understanding of reality.

On December 21, 2012 at 8:45 p.m., a catastrophic event occurred on our planet Earth. The Upstate of South Carolina was one of many areas, in the world, irreparably damaged. There were no living human beings found, within Spartanburg County, after this event.

Although life ended for us, when viewed from one perspective, we soon realized that it continued to thrive in another. Just as you'd hypothesized, in your quantum theory, we eventually came to the realization that the world was filled with unlimited frequencies that offered sentient beings an opportunity to experience an unlimited number of alternate realities.

I remember, like it was yesterday, the feeling I experienced when we discovered that death was not a final nail in a coffin, but rather a chance to change the station on a very large radio.

I've always been in complete awe of your abilities, as a physicist, to be able to understand particle-wave behavior. You were the person responsible for constructing the technology that permitted us to *jump* into another perception of reality. This, in itself, was a small miracle.

When you moved us into a new frequency, in the year, 1973, we always knew that it was extremely important for us to avoid our parallel incarnations that were living out their lives simultaneously in the same reality construct. We agreed, in contract, not to ever contact these individuals. That is, at least, until we'd all passed away. That's the reason the three of us/they cannot access any memories of what has happened. Our agreement not to contact our parallel incarnations within the new perception of reality that we jumped into has precluded us/them from gaining knowledge of the forthcoming event.

The reason I have sent you this letter is because the very scenario, the three of us agreed upon, has now occurred. Kyle and I have passed away into another frequency. You passed away into another frequency many years earlier. I can now send this letter to you (your parallel incarnation, in the year 2000.) The information you are receiving is genuine. The date and time of the event is also accurate.

The schematic drawing of the circuit board that appears on the napkin was drawn by you. You explained to Kyle that it was Tesla technology and that the construction of the circuit board was necessary in order to allow us to be able to *jump* to the next frequency in 1973.

The numbers on top of the napkin, running left to right, represent the longitude and latitude coordinates for the meteorite's point of impact, the date of the event and, of course, the time the impact will occur.

The frequency loop you are currently experiencing recurs indefinitely. It was designed, like all frequencies, so that human beings could experience certain scenarios while learning valuable lessons that could not be attained in other venues.

It is important that you meet Kyle Wilson and Angel McClure at the University of South Carolina Upstate campus on Saturday, December 22, 2012. They will meet you in the Horace C. Smith Science Building at 2:00 in the afternoon. The rest of the journey will be up to you.

I wish you all the luck in the world and hope that your perception of reality will fulfill your higher self's ultimate purpose!

With affection,
Angel McClure—Wilson

Angel folded the letter and gently stuffed it back inside the envelope. She looked at Kyle who was staring at Paul. She felt as if she had been cast into a scene from *The Twilight Zone*.

Paul approached Angel and Kyle. "It's our destiny to jump to another frequency. I have the necessary equipment to accomplish this." He was pointing to the circuit board and television hookup that was situated about 30 feet away.

"What about us?" Annie asked suddenly feeling left out. She'd been referring to Adam, Henry, and herself. They weren't mentioned in Angel's letter to Paul.

Paul hugged Annie. "All of us will make the *jump,* and so will any survivors living in Spartanburg County," he explained.

"Paul, what do you think would happen if we didn't use the Tesla technology?" Kyle asked. He was staring out into the advancing fogbank. "More important, what do you think has happened to the poor souls that disappeared into thin air?"

The skin on Paul's forehead wrinkled a bit as he thought long and hard about Kyle's question. "If we did absolutely nothing, at all, our current reality base would probably disintegrate. We'd most likely mass reincarnate into another reality construct. I believe that's happening to some people already."

"Paul!" Angel interrupted the professor's deep train of thought. "I think we need to act sooner than later. That wall of fog, over there, isn't getting any smaller and it looks, to me, like it's getting a lot closer to us by the minute. We shouldn't be wasting valuable time."

Paul looked up and stared deeply into the fogbank. Angel's advice seemed to refocus his attention. "You're absolutely right, Angel. It's time for us to get rid of that large cumulus cloud, once and for all!"

Chapter Thirty-four

Once again, the professor had his hands clasped tightly around the joystick. Adam and Henry were positioned in front of the television. Annie and Angel were situated a few steps behind them, and Kyle was stationed alongside Paul.

Paul changed the position the satellite dish was facing. He'd given considerable thought, over the years, about what direction to point the receiver, in order to achieve a time *jump* to the year 1973.

In looking over the schematic that his parallel incarnate had drawn, Paul noticed that there were three numbers, *1-6-6*, printed on the bottom of the drawing. Although they'd been incorporated into the body of the diagram, he was thoroughly convinced that these numbers had absolutely nothing to do with the circuit board's construction. The longer he thought about them, the more certain he became that the numbers were, in fact, satellite coordinates the former professor had left behind so that he could point the receiving dish in the proper direction to achieve a successful *jump*. Why he didn't just spell it out, like everything else, had been a mystery to Paul for many years.

Paul figured that the three numbers referred to the longitude coordinates for a communications satellite. After performing some basic research, a few years back, he discovered that the location, 166 degrees E. longitude, was occupied by a retired satellite owned by the company, *Intelsat*. This particular satellite had been launched into space in the mid 1960's. It had been deactivated after a few years of service. Paul learned that the *Intelsat satellite* had since been retired, but it still remained in its original orbit.

Paul calculated that the satellite was positioned in a geostationary orbit, directly above the Earth's equator at 0° latitude. Geostationary satellites appeared motionless in the sky. The professor understood that this was an important factor because the only coordinate he needed to be concerned with, in order to lock the receiving dish on the target, was the longitude calculation. There were various Intelsat satellites and they all differed in their locations by longitude alone.

Paul didn't completely understand why his parallel had honed in on that specific satellite, but he understood the writing on the wall. That's where the former professor had aimed his receiver. Maybe he'd picked up some remnant transmissions from the probe that had an affiliation with the year 1973, or perhaps it was an area in the great vastness of space that he'd stumbled onto, by dumb luck, that offered a portal to that time period. Either way, it was going to provide them with the platform they'd need to activate the *jump*. As long as the final result was achieved, Paul didn't care, at this point, about the reason, why, it was going to work.

Paul had figured a clever way to calculate the longitude coordinate against the backdrop of the sky. He could do it blindfolded without the use of any equipment. He'd used a mental joystick, in his mind's eye, many times before to practice maneuvering the satellite dish into the proper direction. Under normal conditions, the small receiving dish, they'd setup, would not be able to pick up anything useful from the Intelsat satellite. But Paul had to keep reminding himself over and over again, that these were not normal conditions. The millions of frequencies, inside the fogbank, were creating an altogether different environment, on this particular day, which was both highly unusual and quite unstable.

When Paul was completely satisfied that the dish was locked onto the proper coordinate, he placed the joystick back on the ground. He made his way over to the electronic amplifier and picked up the circuit board. It was time for Tesla's technology to do its job. All of his preparations; deciphering the schematic from the napkin; the time and energy he invested building the device, and the tremendous risk he undertook to conceal his secret, were about to payoff. Paul was ready to power up the circuit board.

Chapter Thirty-five

A small, green light flickered to life after Paul pushed a button on the right hand corner of the amplifier board. The light indicated that the circuit board was working.

The television set was back to displaying a blizzard of electronic snow across its screen. The six of them huddled together, in a circle, near the TV as they waited for something magnificent to happen.

"Is it working, Paul?" Angel asked. She was staring at the circuit board.

Paul was looking very intently at the fogbank, off in the distance. "It's working," he proclaimed. "It'll take a little while to harness all the frequencies into the region."

"What exactly is that contraption of yours going to do?" Annie asked. She moved away from the others and walked up to the television. "I was hoping we'd be able to catch some more up-to-the-minute news from SNN."

183

"The way that it works...," Paul said as he turned to face Annie, "...is that the fogbank, over there, acts as a barrier that protects and separates one reality from another. Because our current state of existence is no longer active, the fogbank is providing a natural barrier that prevents us from communicating with anyone outside of Spartanburg County.

"The fogbank, if left alone, would eventually absorb everything that's remaining in our current understanding of reality. We're, in a sense, cheating the system by focusing the satellite dish onto an area that opens a direct pathway into our county. Once I locked onto the satellite, a few minutes ago with the receiving dish, the pathway became active. It's almost like I've completed an electrical circuit and now a free flow of electrons is pouring into Spartanburg County. The frequencies, which are abundant within the fogbank, can now begin to seep into our location because we have created the proper route for them to follow. The amplifier board will boost the intensity of those frequencies a million times. All of this is happening right now."

Annie looked over at Kyle and Angel. She was wearing a frown and wondering if they were as confused as she was. "Paul, about how long will it take for this so called *jump* to occur?" She had her arms folded, openly displaying her growing impatience with the entire process.

Paul glanced up from the circuit board. He turned his attention to the television set that was still broadcasting a snowy picture. "Everybody please move away from the TV," he yelled.

"Now what are you worried about?" Annie asked. She turned to face the TV and didn't notice anything strange occurring.

"Please get away from the TV, right now," he yelled again.

Kyle and Angel each grabbed one of Annie's arms and pulled her gently, in the opposite direction, away from the TV.

Henry and Adam moved backward as well and took a position next to Kyle, Angel, and Annie.

Suddenly, there was a loud pop and a bright flash of light became visible from the back of the television. A few seconds later, some white smoke escaped from the appliance's side panels. The television's screen went from electronic snow to a blank picture as if the unit had been switched off.

"What just happened?" Kyle asked. He stared at the professor. Paul's shirt was hanging out of his brown pants on one side and was still tucked in on the other.

"The process has begun, Kyle." The professor was grinning. He was obviously pleased with the fact that he'd just blown up the last working television set in the entire county. Then his grin widened. "We have about four hours, at the most, before things really begin to get pretty strange around here."

"I think things have been pretty damn strange around here ever since Friday night," Annie said.

Kyle looked at his watch. It was 2 o'clock in the afternoon. "So it's working? We did it?" he asked.

"Yes, my boy, we have initiated the process. The *jump* will occur in about four hours!"

"What are we supposed to do in the mean time?" Adam asked.

Paul turned to face the deputy and his pilot friend. "We're going to need to get out of here. Henry, you'll need to fly us back to Kyle's Apartment complex as soon as possible."

The pilot nodded and began running over to the chopper.

"What about all of this equipment?" Adam asked. "Is it safe to leave it?"

"The equipment served a very useful purpose, but we no longer need it," Paul explained. "Nothing can stop the process once it begins."

Henry had made his way inside the chopper and started the aircraft's engine. The huge blades were already kicking up the loose stones and dirt along the sides of the interstate.

"Please, let's hurry!" Paul urged them. "We need to get back to the apartment complex and get everything organized before 6 o'clock this evening."

Chapter Thirty-six

On board the helicopter, the professor began explaining what they were likely to experience within the next several hours. Once again, they were sporting their blue head sets so that they could all hear one another over the roar of the helicopter's engine.

"Before the *jump* occurs, we should be in close proximity to one another," Paul said. "You have to understand that I, like the five of you, have never experienced this phenomenon before. All of my experience, with this thing, has been limited to mathematical calculations and a lot of theoretical simulations that were based on Quantum Theory."

"What do you think will happen to our personal property?" Angel asked.

Paul's right eyebrow arched slightly. "What you're wearing or holding will, most likely, make the *jump* with you," he said. "Anything else will probably be left behind. I'm really not sure how that will play out. I guess we'll learn a lot more when we go through the actual process?"

"Look at the sky around us," Adam said. He was pointing outside the cockpit. The normally light blue sky had been replaced with a much deeper, purple color. The color of the sky appeared similar to what you'd expect to see while wearing a pair of very strong sunglasses.

"Is that part of the process?" Annie asked.

Paul nodded. "Yes. I believe we'll see the entire sky change its color quite a bit as the flow of frequencies begins infiltrating the area."

As they made their way back into the city limits of Spartanburg, and eventually into the surrounding area near Kyle's apartment complex, the sky took on the unusual color of sea foam green. It was the prettiest looking scene that Angel had ever witnessed.

Henry landed the chopper right on top of Kyle's apartment complex parking lot. He'd found a spot that looked pretty safe.

"Do you two gentlemen have any family members that you'll need to rescue?" Paul asked.

Henry smiled. "I have a wife and a child. I'll attempt to ride this thing out with them, at our house."

"I'll stay with Henry," Adam said. He extended his arm to shake Paul's hand.

Paul shook the hands of both men. "Good luck, fellows. Remember to keep your family members close to one another at all times. If possible, hold hands and sit in a circle before the *jump* occurs. I'm sorry that I can't pinpoint an exact time when this thing will take place. Keep watching the sky. The darker the sky, the closer we'll be to the *jump*. My best estimate is sometime after 6 o'clock.

"After it occurs, things are going to look very strange. We'll probably have about a six hour window of time, following the *jump*, where everything will be empty throughout the entire county. The only people we'll be able to see, during that stretch of time, will be those individuals that make the *jump* with us. After the process has run its course, time has to catch up. We won't see the rest of civilization until six hours later."

"That's a pretty strange concept, Professor," Henry said.

Paul nodded. "That's the way it turned out in every model I've researched. We should use those six hours very wisely. I suggest that we get our bearings, acclimate to our new surroundings, and attempt to procure essential assets such as food and water. Remember, we'll have jumped 39 years into the past. We won't have access to money or credit cards, in 1973. If anything is available, in the way of essentials, during that six hour window of time, I'd be sure to grab it."

"Is there anything else we should know?" Adam asked.

Paul smiled. "Just keep in mind that there's no guarantee that we'll end up in the year 1973. We could, hypothetically, end up in another time and place altogether. Be ready to adapt to whatever venue you find yourselves in."

"I understand," Adam said.

The six of them exchanged goodbyes, hugs, and tears before Kyle, Angel, Annie and Paul exited the chopper.

Henry carefully lifted the helicopter away from the parking lot. Kyle and the others watched as the aircraft quickly moved to a higher altitude and raced across the sky, out of view.

Chapter Thirty-seven

The color of the sky had changed from blue; to deep purple; to sea foam green, and to its current presentation, a very light shade of yellow.

While the Earth's atmospheric conditions were rapidly changing by the hour, Kyle and Angel remained busy packing as many essential supplies as possible, into the Chevy. They primarily focused their attention on gathering items such as food and water. Kyle also placed an extra change of clothes in the car's backseat.

Paul and Annie helped out by searching, through Kyle's apartment, for additional items that they thought might be important to have on their upcoming journey.

When they'd finished going through Kyle's apartment, they proceeded down the outside hallway to do the same routine inside Angel's unit. About an hour after that, they drove the Chevy over to Annie's place so that she could pack some essentials.

Kyle and Paul had noticed that there were very few people visible at the apartment complex. In fact, they'd only seen two people since exiting the helicopter, several hours earlier.

Kyle looked at his watch. It was a few minutes after five o'clock in the afternoon. Based on Paul's estimate, he figured that the actual *jump* was fast approaching. He knew that the precious time remaining, before the big event, was dwindling down to a matter of minutes.

As Annie and Angel finished their scavenger hunt through Annie's apartment, Kyle and Paul observed another change in the sky's color. The new look was pumpkin orange.

Out in the distance, Kyle and Paul also witnessed a few bolts of lightning flash across the sky. It was, pretty much, cloud to cloud activity. Occasionally, they spotted a bolt or two arcing, downward, in the direction of the ground. Kyle was surprised, however, that they weren't able to hear the normally anticipated thunder claps that most people came to expect from such electrical storm activity.

"It's getting closer, Kyle," Paul said. "We're less than an hour away."

"Come on, ladies," Kyle yelled out as he spotted Annie and Angel inside the front entranceway of Annie's apartment.

"We're almost finished. Just give us five more minutes," Angel shouted back.

Kyle glanced nervously at his watch.

Paul came up behind him and gently squeezed the top of his shoulders. "We're still okay on time," he assured him. "The electrical activity has just begun. There's going to be a lot more action up there before the main event." The professor was staring intently into the distant horizon.

Angel and Annie finally emerged from the front door to Annie's place and walked up the sidewalk that led to the parking lot.

"We're finished," Angel announced.

"Good," Paul said. "Let's get in the car and head south on Interstate 85."

Kyle steered the Chevy away from the apartment complex and onto a small access road that merged with a county highway. He drove a few miles and turned the car onto the southbound entrance to I-85. As the foursome made their way down the interstate, they encountered a predictable number of abandoned vehicles in both traffic lanes. Unlike before, they did not spot a single pedestrian anywhere on the highway.

As he drove the Chevy, Kyle became lost in deep thought. He was thinking about how strange the past 72 hours had been. Here he was, on Christmas Eve Day, driving on the Interstate with three very close friends that he'd never met prior to the beginning of this awful catastrophe. It certainly wasn't the way he envisioned bringing in the holiday season.

Kyle wasn't the type of man that was used to spending a lot of time with relatives, opening gifts under a Christmas tree. But he did enjoy listening to the holiday music and viewing the pretty colors that his own fiber optic Christmas decoration would cast throughout the apartment living room. Unfortunately, there'd be none of the usual holiday festivities this season.

A large lightning bolt lit up the entire sky directly in front of them. Paul smiled as he watched the electrical storm begin to grow in intensity. Kyle saw the lightning flash too, and it immediately broke his train of thought regarding the Christmas season.

Annie was observing the rather large smile on the professor's face. "Um… Paul, you do realize that we're driving right into the heart of that storm?" She'd turned to look at the physicist who was seated beside her in the backseat.

"Don't be afraid, Annie," Paul replied. "This is all part of the plan. We'll need to drive right into the area where the lightning strikes are the most intense."

Annie smiled at him, and quickly turned to look at Angel in the front seat. She made a funny facial expression that only the English professor could see. Although Annie hadn't uttered a single word, Angel had read her thoughts loud and clear. Annie had obviously convinced herself that Paul was nuts.

Kyle looked at the sky. The lightning was becoming more frequent. In addition to that, the sky was changing its color again. Now it was transitioning from pumpkin orange to dark red. It looked like something out of a late night horror show.

As they continued to drive, the lightning became so frequent that it was hard to determine the amount of time that existed, if any, between the individual bolts. Up ahead, about a hundred yards, a lightning bolt struck the road. A few seconds after that, another struck the top of an abandoned Toyota Camry. The car vanished into thin air.

"Stop the car right here," Paul said.

Kyle slammed on the brakes and the Chevy made a loud screeching sound as the vehicle came to an abrupt stop.

"Paul, that's the first intelligent thing you've said since we got in this damn car," Annie said. She was scared to death of the approaching storm. "You're going to get us all killed, you old fool."

"Annie, try to relax," Paul said as he placed his hands on her lap. "Everything is under control. Nobody is going to die."

As Paul spoke the words to Annie, the lightning bolts began to attack the surface of the highway directly in front of them. Like they were sheets of rain, the brilliant flashes of lightning completely overwhelmed the road. A wall of continuous cloud to ground lightning existed less than 30 yards ahead of them, and that wall was rapidly moving in their direction.

Chapter Thirty-eight

"Don't panic!" Paul said as he tried his best to reassure Annie and the others that everything was still going according to plan. "This is supposed to happen. The electrical storm is how we'll make the *jump*."

The wall of lightning strikes was moving closer to them by the second. Only about 15 yards remained between the relentless march of lightning bolts and the Chevy.

"Paul, are you sure this is safe? I can still turn the car around and get us the hell out of here," Kyle said.

"It's perfectly safe," he replied. "Don't turn the car around." Paul leaned over the front seat and reached towards the steering wheel. He grabbed the ignition keys and turned the engine off.

"Why'd you do that?" Angel asked. She was scared to death at this point.

"There's no turning back, now. It's time for us to make the jump. Everybody calm down, take a deep breath, and join hands," the physicist said.

They quickly grabbed onto each other's hands and watched as the electric light show, outside, intensified. With each passing second, the lightning strikes edged closer to the car.

When the key bolt of lightning finally hit the Chevy, the four friends immediately felt a tingling sensation run throughout the entire length of their bodies. The next thing they knew, the entire vehicle had been bathed in a beautiful white light. Outside the car, they could see the sky transition from dark red to dark black.

Everything around them seemed to move in slow motion for a few seconds and then, out of nowhere, they were suddenly thrust, like a marble being discharged from a slingshot, backwards through time. It felt as if they were traveling a thousand miles per hour.

A million thoughts raced through their minds. It was as if they'd reviewed the highlights from each of their lives in just a matter of seconds. They were all connected now, holding hands, and passing through the fabric of time as a single entity. And as quickly as the adventure had begun, it ended! The Chevy had come to a complete stop.

Chapter Thirty-nine

They'd arrived in a very dark and quiet place. The lack of available lighting had made it difficult to see much of anything in or around the car. The four friends were still tightly clutching each other's hands.

Kyle looked across at Angel who was seated on the passenger side of the car. He could faintly make out her figure in the poor lighting. "Are you okay?" he asked.

"I'm fine." Angel squeezed his hand a few times to let him know that she was uninjured.

"Paul? Annie? Are you guys alright?" Kyle asked as he turned to face the back seat.

"I'm still in one piece," Annie replied. "What in the world happened?"

"I think that was Paul's *jump*," Angel said.

Kyle tightened his grip around Paul's hand. "That was one hell of a ride. Was it pretty much what you'd anticipated?"

There was no response from the professor.

Kyle quickly turned back to look at Angel. "Can you please get some light in here?"

Angel reached over from the passenger seat and twisted a knob on the front dashboard. The Chevy's dome light, above them, immediately provided soft, white light inside the vehicle.

As soon as Kyle turned back around to check on Paul, he'd realized that something was terribly wrong with his friend. "Paul, can you hear me? Paul, wakeup! I think we've made the *jump*." Kyle reached over the front seat and grabbed the professor's shirt with both his hands. He shook him several times without getting a response.

Paul was sitting in the back seat, slumped over on his right side, with both eyes shut. His skin had lost its vibrancy and appeared pale.

Kyle placed his two fingers on the physicist's neck and checked for a pulse. He didn't sense one. Looking down at his friend, he thought to himself that the older man's heart must have given out from the stress associated with the ordeal they'd just gone through. He reasoned that somewhere between the years 2012 and 1973, Paul had probably entered another perception of reality.

Chapter Forty

Annie stared at Kyle. She was visibly upset. "Is he going to be alright?"

Kyle looked up from the professor and focused his attention on Annie. He was wearing a somber expression across his face. "Annie, I don't think Paul was strong enough to make the *jump*."

Annie had tears streaming down the sides of her cheeks. Her face was beat red. "He can't be dead, Kyle, he just can't be. We need him to tell us what to do. Damn you, Paul. You're the reason why we're all here in the first place. You told me, not even five minutes ago, that nobody was going to die." She reached over and shook him really hard. The professor's head was shaking back and forth like a bobble head doll.

"Calm down," Angel yelled as she reached over the back seat and placed her hands on Annie's shoulders. She tried to comfort her friend the best way she knew how.

Suddenly, the professor let out a large gurgling cough. It came from deep within his lungs and was followed by a loud wheezing sound that originated from inside the physicist's chest cavity. Kyle, Angel, and Annie were startled by the new signs of life exhibited by their, thought to be fallen, friend. The professor's face gradually began to regain its color and his eyes fluttered a few times before they popped open. Paul's entire body convulsed for a few moments before it straightened in the back seat. "Whatever you do, Kyle, don't turn the car around," he yelled out. He was staring at his friends looking completely disoriented.

Annie reached out and threw her arms around him. "Thank god you're alive. I thought you left us, you old fool."

"What a relief," Angel sighed. "Paul, you scared the living daylights out of us."

Kyle was grinning broadly at the professor. "What happened, Paul? Do you remember anything, at all?"

Paul looked at his friends like they were completely crazy. "What are you guys talking about? Did we make the jump?"

Kyle looked at Angel. "I can't believe that he slept through the most important event in his life."

Angel smiled at Kyle and reached over to give him a big hug. "I'm just glad that he's awake right now, when it counts."

Chapter Forty-one

The level of lighting gradually improved outside the Chevy. Although the viewing conditions were not completely perfect, Kyle could now see that they were still positioned on the interstate highway. As his eyes continued to acclimate to the outside world, he recognized the exact location they currently occupied. They were approximately fifty yards from the exit that led to the Hearon Circle. This was an area, near the I-85 Interstate system, that connected a number of Spartanburg County roads to the larger interstate tributary.

Paul looked out the back seat window. He also recognized where they were at. He could tell by the highway's layout, and the surrounding buildings, that they were no longer in the year 2012. He'd remembered the scene, he was currently observing, very well from looking at countless photographs of Spartanburg County during the 1970's. He'd viewed the pictures, in the public library, many times in preparation for his eventual journey to this time period and location.

"Is this the exit to the Asheville Highway?" Annie asked. She'd remembered being on this particular road many times in the past.

"I believe that's the Hearon Circle in front of us," Angel said. She was suddenly very excited by her recognition of familiar looking landmarks.

"We're actually here," Paul said. He had, pretty much, recovered from his near death experience. "We've made it to the year, 1973!"

Kyle attempted to start the car. In his mind, he crossed the fingers on both hands as he turned the ignition key. The Chevy's engine started on the first try. He placed the gearshift into drive and maneuvered the vehicle onto the exit that was directly in front of them. As the car slowly made its way down the exit ramp, they passed a Howard Johnson's Motel on the right side of the road. They drove a little farther and passed a Dairy Barn Ice Cream stand and finally came to a McDonald's restaurant. Kyle pulled the car into the McDonald's parking lot.

The lights, in the restaurant, were on but there was no sign of additional activity taking place. It was getting lighter by the minute. Kyle could tell that it was going to be a beautiful sunny day. Out in the distant, western horizon, he could see the familiar looking contour of the mountains.

They exited the automobile and walked up to the restaurant's front entrance. Paul pulled at the door. It was unlocked and they were able to walk inside. As soon as they did so, they smelled the inviting aroma of breakfast food and coffee. Besides them, the restaurant appeared entirely vacant.

Annie walked up to the front counter where the cash registers were positioned. As she peered into the back section of the store, she quickly noticed that the food trays were filled with, already wrapped, packages of McDonald's products. Annie briefly eyed Angel before she hoisted her large body over the short counter. She landed safely on the other side.

"What are you doing?" Angel asked, amused by Annie's actions.

"I'm going to get some breakfast. I've not had anything to eat in over 39 years." Annie picked up a package of hash browns. The golden crusty flakes of potato were hot and smelled incredibly good. She cautiously tasted the food and smiled at Angel and the others. "This is absolutely fantastic. I highly recommend that we place a large order right now while the lines are extremely short."

Angel climbed over the counter and began helping Annie to place the packages of breakfast food inside some *to go bags* that they'd found stacked underneath the cooking grill.

Paul looked at Kyle and smiled. "I don't know about you, but I'm pretty hungry as well."

"But, how do we pay for this stuff?" Kyle asked as he turned to look at Annie and Angel. He'd brought up the obvious question, which dealt with ethics and morality, nobody wanted to discuss.

Paul walked up to Kyle and gently consoled his conscience. "First of all, there's no one here to pay. Second, we have a little over five hours remaining to be able to stock up on some supplies and money. After that, life in the year 1973 is going to resume."

Kyle glanced at Angel and Annie. He smiled and said, "What the hell, it's not like we've been able to control what's happened to us."

Kyle carefully examined a cash register that had been resting on the countertop. He located and pushed a button on its key pad that had the word *DRAWER* printed on it. As soon as he did so, the cash register's bottom drawer opened revealing a fully stocked tray of five, ten, and twenty dollar bills. Kyle reached over and cleaned out the entire drawer. There were five other registers and he repeated the same process of opening the drawers and cleaning out the cash in each of them.

When they finally made it back inside the Chevy, they had taken enough McDonald's food to feed an army. Kyle had taken over eleven hundred dollars from the fast food restaurant. Although he felt badly about stealing the money, he rationalized that this was the only course of action that would allow them to have an opportunity to get back on their feet once civilization returned to normal in a few hours.

In his mind, Kyle had made a decision to anonymously return every dollar he'd stolen from the McDonald's restaurant once he was settled, and earning a decent living.

Kyle drove the Chevy back onto the interstate. It was clear sailing and there were no signs of any abandoned cars on the highway. They continued driving for several hours south on I-85. They passed right through the perimeter line that had previously imprisoned them within the 30 mile area. They saw no signs of a white fogbank or any wide scale destruction that might have originated from Friday night's catastrophic event. They had truly arrived in the year, 1973.

Their plan was to drive as far away from Spartanburg County as possible. They wanted to make sure that Paul and Annie had absolutely zero chances of running into their parallel selves from the year 1973. That meant driving the Chevy all the way down to the state of Florida.

Several hours later, Paul tapped on Kyle's shoulder from the back seat. "I think we should pull over and rest for awhile," he said. "According to my calculations, the six hour period is just about up. We don't want to be driving around on the interstate when people, and other vehicles, begin transitioning back into our perception of reality."

Kyle looked at Paul, in the rear view mirror, and nodded. He slowly decreased the car's speed and parked the vehicle on the roadside. They were about 25 miles north of Florida.

Annie, Angel, and Paul were seated in the car, still snacking on McDonald's food, waiting for the rest of civilization to catch up with them.

Kyle was completely exhausted. He just wanted to close his eyes and drift off to sleep. He tried to fight the urge to sleep, but the amount of exhaustion he'd been battling, for the past several days, was beginning to overtake him.

Angel could tell that he was tired. She ran her fingers through his long blond hair a few times and smiled. "Why don't you rest your eyes for a little while? I'll wake you if something important happens."

"It's a deal," he said with a large grin plastered across his face. Kyle closed his eyes. He was extremely happy. They had made it out of Spartanburg alive. At last, he could let his guard down just a bit and relax. Kyle Wilson was finally able to have what he craved more than anything else in the world – some much needed sleep.

Chapter Forty-two

Kyle drifted into a very deep sleep. It was one of the most prolonged periods of rest he'd experienced in several months. After awhile, he sensed his body gently floating above the parked Chevy. Suddenly, he was being propelled through time again. Only now he was moving at breakneck speed in the opposite direction. Kyle was moving forward, in time, and heading back to the future. He experienced the feeling of moving extremely fast for, what seemed like, several minutes. And as suddenly as it had begun, the sensation of moving forward stopped.

When he awoke from his restful slumber, Kyle was seated on the Italian leather recliner inside his living room apartment. He rubbed at his eyes and glanced at various locations throughout the apartment. Everything looked the way it always did. The television was playing in the background; his laptop computer was in hibernation mode, but still running. Kyle was disoriented. He stood up from the recliner and walked around the small apartment. He glanced at his watch. It was 8:30 in the evening and, according to the timepiece, the date was December 21, 2012.

He couldn't believe it. It wasn't possible. He'd, apparently, dozed off in the recliner and dreamt the entire tale. It had been nothing more than a dream. The entire thing had happened in a matter of minutes. Kyle had manufactured this crazy story inside his brain. None of it actually happened. There'd been no catastrophic event; no fogbank; no professor Paul Grossman; no Angel McClure. Yet, in his mind, it had all seemed so very real.

Gradually, his head began to clear and the dream began to make more sense to him. First, he'd bumped into the pretty girl, at the rental office, and immediately placed her on a pedestal. He'd imagined her to be this metaphorical angel that was missing from his life. She was the missing ornament from his Christmas tree. While picking up her things from off the ground, he'd noticed that she'd been carrying an English textbook and so, naturally, he made her an English professor in his totally ridiculous fantasy.

And there was Paul, the professor from the university. There was no professor, Paul Grossman. There was only, Paul Callahan, the maintenance guy at the Brimstone Apartment Complex. He was the guy Kyle could always count on to fix various items around the apartment. Kyle smiled. He'd made the maintenance guy, the fixer of many things in real life, a physics professor in the dream. Where did he ever get a silly idea like that from? He looked up at the television. The movie, *Back to the Future* was still playing in the background. He chuckled a bit. "The time travel theme, the parents, the kid manipulating the future," he said softly to himself as he shook his head in disbelief. In his dream, he'd even incorporated the concept of him having an imaginary son, named James, with the pretty brunette.

There was also Annie Hendricks; the very real person that worked for the apartment complex. She was in charge of collecting rent from the tenants that lived on the property. It was all coming together now.

Kyle looked on the floor alongside the recliner. The December issue of *Time Magazine* was folded open to the story about the doomsday event known as December 21, 2012. It was a lengthy article he'd been reading about the end of the Mayan Calendar and how various scholars had predicted a catastrophic event would occur on that date which, by coincidence, happened to be today. Kyle picked up the magazine and leafed through the seven pages that had been dedicated to the story. On page 46, right in the middle of the article, was a big advertisement for the Chevrolet Company. There was a large commemorative picture of a yellow, 1973, Chevy Chevelle that had been completely restored by a guy that lived in the state of Indiana. *What an imagination I must have*, he thought to himself.

When he finally cleared the cobwebs from his head, Kyle washed his face in the bathroom sink before returning to the living room. He suddenly had the biggest craving, ever, for McDonald's food. *Why not*, he thought.

He reached for the car keys, on the dining room table, and headed for the front door. Suddenly, there was a knock at the door. He stopped in his tracks and looked down at his watch; it was exactly 8:45 p.m. A bit of a chill worked its way through his entire body. He wasn't expecting anyone. Kyle hesitated for a moment before opening the door.

The pretty brunette he'd bumped into at the rental office, two days earlier, was standing in front of him.

"Hi Kyle, I'm Kelly Hansen, your new neighbor from across the hall," the girl said.

Kyle couldn't believe his eyes. Angel McClure was about to walk back into his life. He stared at her for a few seconds. She was as beautiful as any angel he'd ever imagined.

"I didn't get a chance to thank you the other day for helping me pick up my things," she explained. "You left in such a hurry. I hope you don't mind, but I got the lady, Annie, in the rental office to give me your name and apartment number."

Kyle kept smiling at the pretty girl. "No. Uh, I don't mind at all. Come inside Ange..." He caught himself just as he started to call her Angel. "Come inside, Kelly," he said. Kyle watched her walk into the living room. "Can I offer you something to drink?"

She blushed slightly as she casually looked around the apartment. "If you have some bottled water, that'd be great."

He closed the front door. "Wait right here for a second, Kelly." Kyle walked across the room and into his kitchen. As he reached for the last two bottles of Deer Park water inside the refrigerator door, he heard a loud thunderous boom outside the apartment. The noise was followed by another; an all too familiar screeching sound that seemed to tear a massive hole in the Earth's atmosphere. Kyle ran out into the living room clutching the bottled waters. He looked at Kelly who was staring back at him. A look of uncertainty was etched on her face. Their eyes suddenly connected and became locked on one another. The screeching noise outside continued to grow louder.

As Kyle and Kelly continued to stare into each other's eyes, a strange feeling of déjà vu overtook them. The sensation made them relax and they became less concerned about the horrific noise coming from outside the apartment.

Kyle thought, for a moment, about Paul's quantum theory regarding alternate realities and particle-wave behavior. What if the adventure hadn't been a dream after all? What if they'd tapped into another frequency and were currently experiencing an alternate form of reality? Kyle smiled at Kelly, studying the familiarity of her beautiful face, before she disappeared into the darkness. The lights had just gone out!

Perimeter

John Reizer

www.ingramcontent.com/pod-product-compliance
Lightning Source LLC
Chambersburg PA
CBHW031109260626
47172CB00001B/289